MARIE FERRARELLA

In His Protective Custody

ROMANTIC
SUSPENSE

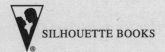

SILHOUETTE BOOKS

ISBN-13: 978-0-373-27714-8

IN HIS PROTECTIVE CUSTODY

Copyright © 2011 by Marie Rydzynski-Ferrarella

Visit Silhouette Books at www.eHarlequin.com

Printed in U.S.A.

Books by Marie Ferrarella

MARIE FERRARELLA

This *USA TODAY* bestselling and RITA® Award-winning author has written two hundred books for Silhouette and Harlequin Books, some under the name of Marie Nicole. Her romances are beloved by fans worldwide. Visit her website at www.marieferrarella.com.

To Nik, whom I loved and was proud of
from the first moment I laid eyes on him

Chapter 1

Despite graduating from medical school in the top five percent of her class, which required endless hours of studying and hands-on experience, Dr. Aleksandra Pulaski didn't think that the human body could sink to this level of exhaustion and still function.

Yet hers had and it still worked.

In her mind, her consciousness amounted to a modern-day miracle of minor proportions. Now, finally at the end of her endless day, she managed to put one foot in front of the other and drag herself from the underground parking structure to the elevator of the building she'd just moved into this month. The trip from the elevator to the front door of her apartment seemed twice as long as it should have been. Almost at journey's end—every foot counted—she managed to get her key into the lock and get inside the incredibly spacious three-bedroom apartment without collapsing.

That was when the last of her energy evaporated. Even the fumes on which she'd been running were gone. Just like that, her knees gave out.

Fortunately, she was passing the sofa in the living room when they buckled. Angling, she landed on top of a cushion, utterly unable to move.

She took it as an omen. Mama was very big on omens and, although normally she'd pretended it was all just old-country nonsense whenever her mother, Paulina Pulaski, brought up the subject, a very tiny part of her was her mother's daughter and believed in omens.

Right now, she would have believed in the existence of unicorns and pixies if it meant that she could just lie here for a few moments. Just long enough to gather her strength for the long trek from the living room to the second bedroom. That was the one she had claimed as her own once she stopped protesting that she couldn't accept such a generous offer. The people making the offer were her cousins. They were the ones who actually lived here.

Or *had* lived here before all five had gotten married. The protest was composed of one part honor and two parts guilt, both sections fueled by the fact that no one would allow her to pay even a small portion of the lease on this perfectly located fifth-floor apartment.

Her cousins, doctors all, had said that she was doing them a favor, watching over the apartment when they weren't around. Her fortuitous arrival in New York City had been the deciding factor that had them all agreeing to continue the lease on the apartment. At least, they would have somewhere to crash when they found themselves too tired to make the drive home to Queens or to the Island.

Alyx quickly discovered that they, Sasha, Natalya, Kady, Tania and Marja, were all one nicer than the other. They divided the cost of the lease among themselves, leaving her to reap the benefits of their generosity. All they required was that she live in the apartment and occasionally dust if she had the time.

She wished she and her three sisters had gotten to know her cousins better, like when they were all growing up. They would have, she was fairly confident, if Papa had lived.

But after that awful day when Papa was taken from them, Mama had pretended that Uncle Josef and his family didn't exist. She absolutely refused to allow any one of them to even get in contact with this branch of the family—the only family they had outside of one another and their aunt Zofia. Mama had never explained why, but Alyx was certain that it had to do with Papa's death. Mama had changed abruptly right after Papa had died in that freak accident. Someone—the police had never been able to find out who—had accidentally pushed Papa, a transit cop, onto the tracks as he waited for the train.

Horrified and heartbroken, Mama held everyone, including the City of New York and Uncle Josef who had initially sponsored Papa's passage to America, accountable for his death. Five days after the funeral, Mama had uprooted all of them and moved to Chicago, where her sister, Aunt Zofia, lived.

She'd said it was because she needed help in raising four girls without a husband to support her. It had been an excuse to turn her back on her husband's family. Her decision was final, and for close to twenty years, she refused to discuss it or even have that side of the family's names mentioned. In return, her mother devoted herself to the four of them. When Aunt Zofia passed away from leukemia, she left her money to the four of them and Mama.

That was when she discovered that her secretive aunt held the title of a popular patent that had yielded a fortune, all of which was banked. Subsequently, a substantial amount of money, even in these dire times, was accrued. It turned out to be enough money to send all of them through college and whatever postgraduate school they chose to attend. They all picked medical school.

Or rather, it was picked for them. Mama would not hear of any of them being anything else. Fortunately, they all felt the calling. Or at least three of them did. It had taken Krystyna a bit longer to come around.

And still there had been no attempt on Mama's part to seal the rift that she had created.

When Alyx told her mother that she'd been accepted by Patience Memorial Hospital to complete her residency, the older woman finally, grudgingly, came around enough to get in touch with Uncle Josef and Aunt Magda.

Luckily, when it came to grudges, her aunt and uncle were as different from her mother as night was day. One phone call later she had family here. Family that embraced her and made the scary transition from Illinois to New York so much easier. The ordeal she had envisioned for herself, living with five other roommates in some small, rundown apartment with hot and cold running roaches, was no longer a viable threat.

She'd been awestruck the first time she'd walked into the apartment her five cousins had lived in during their medical training. Her cousins had all laughed at her expression of wonder, but it wasn't at her expense. There was a joyfulness to it that she quickly came to expect from these women whose blood was the same as hers. These women who were all on their way to becoming highly respected physicians in their chosen fields.

As quickly as she came to love them, she was still more than a little in awe. They were all admirable women.

Maybe that was why Mama had been so adamant about all four of them becoming doctors. Growing up, there had been no other course to follow, no other careers even to consider. Mama wouldn't allow it. Her girls, she'd said time and again, were going to become doctors no matter what the cost. Thanks to Aunt Zofia, there was no amassed debt to face.

But even if Aunt Zofia had been a pauper, the course of their lives had been laid out. Mama had spoken.

Though she loved the woman dearly—they all did—Alyx knew, as did her sisters, that Mama had an obsessive, highly competitive side to her. And that competitiveness always involved the daughters of Papa's older brother.

Her cousins, bless them, were nothing like she'd expected—and turned out to be everything that she needed. Instantly friendly, instantly warm, their combined support made her first day at Patience Memorial not utterly terrible. The latter condition was purely the results of the mentor she'd been assigned. Her first rotation was in the ER with a martinet who shouted rather than talked, put down rather than lifted up.

Rumor had it the woman wanted to get the very best out of her and the other residents assigned the ER rotation. That was the rumor. However, Alyx secretly felt that Dr. Gloria Furst enjoyed putting people down and trampling on their self-esteem.

Alyx refused to let the doctor demoralize her, but it was still an exhausting, draining experience. Four weeks into the rotation and Alyx caught herself praying that the chief of staff or someone else in power would come by unannounced to witness the woman's M.O.

But prayer or no prayer, that was not about to happen. Dr. Furst had a network going for her comprised of residents who would do *anything* not to wash out of the program. Consequently, to cull her favor they clued her in when they heard anything and Dr. Furst *always* knew when someone of stature within the hospital's hierarchy would be stopping by.

It was at that point that the woman went from being the maniacal Mr. Hyde to the kindly Dr. Jekyll. She became sweet enough to send any diabetic in a ten-mile radius into a coma.

This too shall pass, Alyx told herself as she stretched out on the sofa.

Two shifts. She'd endured two full, back-to-back shifts. How in heaven's name did they think she could be at the top of her game in this life-or-death arena by the end of the second shift when her brain felt numb and the rest of her was on automatic pilot? She was lucky she hadn't killed anyone, she thought with a huge, soul-felt sigh that seemed to all but deplete her.

She was running on empty.

Alyx realized that her eyes were closed.

Two minutes, she promised herself. Two minutes and then she'd get up. That's all she needed, just two little…

Her eyes flew open a second before she found solace in sleep.

She strained to listen. Maybe she'd imagined it. Maybe it was just part of the haze that was descending on her brain—

Get back here, you damn bitch! Don't turn your back on me when I'm talking to you! You hear me?

No, definitely not part of her dream, Alyx thought, swinging her legs off the sofa and sitting up. Her brain didn't create scenarios like that, even when it had the freedom of sleep.

The yelling came from her next-door neighbors. Or

rather, from her next-door neighbor. A married couple lived there and what she was hearing was only the man's voice. Hearing it as clearly as if he were in standing in the room with her.

God forbid, Alyx thought with a shiver. Although he was tall and good-looking in a showy kind of way, Harry McBride gave her the creeps.

Harry was shouting at his wife, Abby. Again. As far as she could find out from talking to the doorman, Harry and his wife were new to the building. They had moved in just as Marja had moved out to live with her fiancé—now her husband.

Silence.

Alyx listened for a moment, clinging to the momentary spate of quiet and hoping that it would continue, signaling an end to the abrupt outburst.

Maybe it had just been some kind of heated difference of—

The crash Alyx heard two seconds later followed by a volley of cursing and yelling ushered in a death knell to her sliver of hope. The heart-wrenching, high-pitched yelp of distress was almost too much to bear. She couldn't quite make out what Abby was saying, but the cadence told her that the woman was pleading.

Alyx felt herself growing angry.

Ordinarily, she didn't meddle in other people's lives. Had the noise been generated by an untimely party, she would have put cotton in her ears and gone to her bedroom. She had nothing against people having fun, even the noisy kind.

But this didn't sound like fun. This was a woman in distress.

She'd be distressed, too, living with this Neanderthal. She remembered her first encounter with Harry McBride. It was on the elevator, shortly after she'd moved in. He'd actually hit on her. His wife, Abby, a meek, mousey little thing who seemed almost afraid to raise her all but lifeless eyes from the floor, had been right there, a witness to the encounter. Abby had pretended not to hear.

But she'd heard all right. Alyx would have sworn to it. The woman's face was flushed with embarrassment—all except for one cheekbone which, despite the heavy layer of foundation appeared bluish. As if there was a bruise beneath the coating of makeup, healing.

The yelling continued, the volume swelling.

Alyx shook her head as she walked out into the hallway. The apartment on the other side of the McBrides was vacant so she was the only one privy to this "Punching Judy" show.

Alyx knocked on the door once, then again, harder this time to be heard above Harry's voice. She raised her own as she called out, "Abby, is everything all right in there?"

Instead of Abby, it was her husband who answered the question, punctuating his words with what sounded like a snarl.

"Everything's just fine. Now why don't you mind your own damn business?"

She was a doctor. Alyx thought, struggling to rein in

her anger. As far as she was concerned, humanity *was* her business. And this surly neighbor had just crossed the line with her.

But angry as she was, Alyx had no desire to become the man's next punching bag. So instead of demanding entrance to their apartment, she went into her own, closed the door and waited.

She didn't have long to wait.

The shouting and noise started up within less than five minutes. Round two was even worse and more vitriolic. Whatever had incurred the man's wrath the first time around was still there. And growing.

Alyx dialed 911.

"Hey, Calloway," Sgt. Stubbs called out. "You just caught one."

Officer Zane Calloway—all six foot two of him— kept on walking toward the front door. He knew he couldn't pretend not to hear, but it was worth a shot. Sarge just shouted louder.

"I'm off duty," Zane called back to the desk sergeant.

"Not for another seven minutes," the desk sergeant countered, pointing to the large clock that hung on the wall behind him. "C'mon back, Calloway. I don't want to have to put you on report for failing to obey a higher-ranking authority."

Zane didn't bother suppressing a sigh as he turned around. The white-haired sergeant had earned the right to pull rank. For the most part, Stubbs was a decent, fair man. But Zane was tired and he just wanted to go home and get something to eat.

Or maybe to drink to wash away the taste of the day. He'd had a kid die on him today, a fifteen-year-old who had everything to live for and no reason to die except that he'd been in the wrong place at the wrong time when an inebriated driver had lost control of his vehicle. Zane was in no mood to be accommodating.

"Have a heart, Sarge. I pulled a double shift because Martinez's wife had her baby three days early. Technically, I was off duty hours ago."

The sergeant looked at him over the rim of his reading glasses. It was that "no-nonsense" look he gave the rookies. It hadn't intimidated Zane then, and it didn't now.

"I don't deal in 'technically,' Calloway. I deal in phone calls. In good citizens who call in because they need us."

Returning to the desk, Zane rolled his eyes. "Spare me the violins, please."

Stubbs chuckled under his breath. Zane had never known anyone who actually chuckled before, but the sergeant did.

"Don't know what you're missing, Calloway." Stubbs tore off the page on which he'd written both the complaint and the name and address of the person calling in making the compliant and held it out to him. "Here. This is on your way home. A domestic violence case. Neighbor called it in. A Dr. Pul-lass-key," he added, drawing out the name to get it right.

Zane took the piece of paper with the information on it and frowned as he scanned it. Alleged domestic violence cases rubbed him the wrong way, but not for the reason most people would have expected.

"Another neighbor with her ear pressed against the door, trying to hear what's going on," he commented under his breath.

The sergeant heard him. Wide, squat shoulders rose and fell beneath the navy blue shirt in a careless, dismissive gesture. "We get a call, we're obligated to check it out, no matter who it's from."

Zane tucked the piece of paper into his pocket. He glanced at the desk sergeant's craggy face. His work on the streets and four divorces had made Jacob Stubbs look older than his years.

"Easy for you to say," Zane told him, "sitting behind that desk."

Stubbs looked down his Roman nose at him. "That's 'cause I'm the desk sergeant and you're just a lowly officer."

"Not after I pass my exam," Zane reminded him. It had been Stubbs who'd given him the heads up—and the books—about the exams, saying he was too damn smart to spend his days patrolling a beat. After a while, Zane had decided he had nothing to lose by studying. If he didn't feel ready, no one was holding a gun to his head to take the exam.

Never hurt to keep his options open.

"Yeah, the exam," Stubbs echoed with a laugh, knowing nothing goaded the young policeman on more than being dismissed. "I'll believe it when I see it. Until then—" He let his voice trail off as he motioned Zane out the front entrance, his meaning clear.

"Right." Turning on his heel, Zane headed for the door one more time. "Waste of time, you know. Probably just another false alarm."

"Then it won't take long," the sergeant called after him.

Taking out the paper again once he was outside the precinct, Zane glanced at the address. The sergeant was right. It was on his way home and wasn't all that far away, about a mile from Patience Memorial, as he recalled.

Of course, a mile in Manhattan wasn't equal to a mile anywhere else, except maybe in Los Angeles, where the traffic was equally as maddening at any given time, night or day.

Zane headed for the parking structure where he'd left his car.

He'd probably make better time walking, even at this time of night, he reasoned darkly. But he had no intentions of doubling back to the precinct to get his car once he took down the neighbor's report and talked to the couple who were supposedly fighting. No, once he checked this out, he was going to "check out" himself for at least the next eight hours and recharge some very badly depleted batteries.

He'd left his vehicle on the third level. Once he located it, he got in and drove down the serpentine path to the street level. He was impatient to have this behind him.

The traffic gods were kind to him this evening. Vehicles flowed at an even pace and he got to the address the sergeant had handed him in less than half an hour. He parked his car directly before the entrance, much to the apparent displeasure of the doorman, who attempted to point him in the direction of the building's underground parking.

"Won't be here long enough to need underground parking," Zane informed him in his no-nonsense, baritone voice. Deep and resonant, it didn't leave any room for argument from anyone except the most foolish and reckless. Neither of which A.J. Green, the doorman, was. He stepped back as Zane entered the building. "Elevator's on your right, Officer," A.J. called after him.

"I kind of figured that out," Zane commented as he pushed the up button with his thumb.

A minute and a half later he was knocking on the door of apartment 5E. The hall, he noted as he'd walked up to the door, was as silent as a tomb. There was no sound of an argument, heated or otherwise.

Just as he'd expected.

"Who is it?" a soft voice on the other side of the door wanted to know.

"Officer Calloway," he announced. "NYPD." He stepped back two steps so that the woman could verify the information for herself if she looked through the door's peephole. "We received a call from someone reporting some kind of domestic disturbance going on in this building." Try as he might, he couldn't quite manage to keep the annoyance out of his voice. "Was that you?"

Alyx opened the door, expecting to see, given the man's tone, a slightly down at the mouth, scowling police officer. Most likely somewhat paunchy. Definitely not friendly.

What she saw, instead, could have best been described as the answer to every woman under the age of a hundred's fantasy dream man. At the very least, the man for whom the phrase "tall, dark and gorgeous" had been coined.

Because he was.

He was also scowling fit to kill.

Chapter 2

Something about the officer's tone put Alyx on the defensive. She studied his face attentively as she answered his question. "I made the call, yes."

He gestured impatiently around the well-lit hallway with its alabaster walls. "So where is this alleged disturbance?" he asked.

"It *was*—" she emphasized the word because there was nothing but silence in the hallway now "—coming from the apartment next door. 5F," she added in case his sense of direction took him to the apartment on the other side of hers.

He turned his head toward 5F and remained quiet for a moment, straining to listen. Nothing but silence met his ear.

"Sure it wasn't just the television you heard?" he suggested. "Some of the programs on the cable channels can get pretty loud and violent."

Obviously, *he* thought this was the source of the commotion. But Alyx knew what she'd heard and she intended to stand by it, even if Mr. Drop-Dead-Gorgeous-Policeman *was* smirking at her.

"It was the man next door," she told him firmly, then added for good measure, "and he was shouting at his wife."

All right, maybe she *had* heard raised voices, Zane allowed. But that didn't automatically mean that there had to be violence or abuse involved. "Some guys get a little hot under the collar and they don't realize how loud they sound when they shout."

Why was this policeman so adamant about her being wrong about what she'd heard? Was he a friend of Harry's and trying to protect the man?

"There was also banging," Alyx insisted.

"Maybe he slammed a few drawers or cabinet doors to knock off some steam."

"His wife had bruises."

The statement caught him up short. "You saw bruises?" Zane demanded.

Moment of truth, Alyx thought. She could either lie and hopefully get him to go next door to confront the bully, or she could tell the skeptical-looking officer the truth and pray he'd still do the decent thing and question the man next door.

Opening her mouth, Alyx was about to go with the

first choice, but then she stopped. If this policeman caught her in a lie, he'd dismiss her 911 call and everything else she said or would say as merely being a case of an overactive imagination.

So she went with the truth. "Yes. She tried to cover them up with makeup, but black and blue is a hard combination to camouflage if you're looking at a person close up."

"If the domestic violence was in progress when you made the call at—" Zane paused to look at the paper he'd been given to confirm the time "—twelve-fifteen, when would the alleged battered wife have had the time to try to cover the bruises up with makeup?" he asked suspiciously.

She'd hoped not to have to admit to this part. "I saw the last set of bruises. Or what I assume were the last set."

Just as he'd thought. His deep-blue eyes pinned her, leaving no wiggle space whatsoever. "And exactly when was this?"

Her reluctance increased—but she really had no choice. She doled out the information between gritted teeth. "Two weeks ago. In the elevator. He was with her. And she looked very afraid," she stressed. The officer appeared utterly unconvinced. Frustrated, Alyx added, "He came on to me. His wife was standing right there." Didn't he see what a reprehensible reptile Harry was?

"This got under your skin," he theorized. "So are you trying to get back at him now by accusing him of being guilty of domestic abuse?"

How the hell had he gotten that out of what she'd just said?

Her eyes flashed. "I am *not* trying to get back at anyone," she informed him indignantly, struggling to hold on to her frayed temper. "I *am* trying to prevent someone from getting hurt—or worse. I'm a doctor," she informed him. "I know the signs that go with abuse. I also have excellent hearing. He was threatening her—and slapping her around, from the sound of it." She drew herself up, wishing she was taller than her five-foot-four stature. "Now if you don't want to go next door and talk to him, send over someone who will."

The woman was feisty, he'd give her that, Zane thought. Whether or not that was a good quality in this particular case he hadn't made up his mind yet.

"I will talk to him," Zane replied, his voice distant.

It was essentially a matter of crossing his "t's" and dotting his "i's." Otherwise, he would have told her to do whatever she felt she had to do and just walked away.

It wasn't indifference on his part that was the deciding factor in the way he viewed this case. Neither was it that he condoned battery of any kind, whether it was against a wife *or* a husband. But he had seen the extent of damage a false accusation could create, the kind of havoc it could bring about.

He'd lived through it.

In an effort to get sole custody of her children when she divorced his father, Annie Calloway had filed charges of domestic abuse against her husband. *False* charges of domestic abuse. His father, a man he'd idolized from the first moment he drew breath, had been devastated that the woman he loved would have accused him of such a terrible thing.

At first, Jack Calloway fought the charges tooth and nail, but the court sympathized with her and ruled in his mother's favor. Eventually, despondent and drinking heavily, his father wound up losing everything, including his job on the police force. His friends tried to shield him, but Jack was a lost cause. Unable to face what he had become and, more importantly, unable to cope with the emptiness of life without his family, Zane's father killed himself using his service revolver.

His mother was the first to be informed of what had happened. Realizing that she had been instrumental in his death, Annie was never the same. Neither were Zane and his younger brothers. All three of them had a love-hate relationship with their mother that went unchanged until the day she died—a little more than a year ago.

Because of that, because of what his mother had caused to happen and then never attempted to rescind, Zane had trouble trusting women—all women—and was particularly distrustful of reports of domestic abuse. It was far too easy to wield an accusation as a weapon and gain favor with a sympathetic presiding judge.

As he turned to knock on the next door, Zane became aware that the petite blonde had left the shelter of her apartment and was not just out in the hall, but standing right next to him. So close that he could actually smell her perfume. It slipped in and out of his consciousness like a seductive whisper.

That was all he needed, a distracting sidekick. "Afraid you're going to miss some of the show?" he asked her.

She should have brought a sweater with her to prevent getting frostbite. The officer's tone was *that* cold. What *was* his problem?

"I accused him, I should be able to face him," she answered, attempting to approximate the same tone that Calloway had used.

She didn't quite achieve it. Friendliness was more her byword. Cold hostility didn't begin to enter the bargain. She thought of Harry beating his wife, secure in the feeling that no one would challenge him and the coldness came, belatedly.

"Why don't you just wait in your apartment?" Zane suggested crisply. "If there's anything to tell, I'll fill you in when it's over."

When it was over, he'd leave, she thought, fairly confident that she'd pegged the officer's mode of operation. He was the type to only keep the promises he deemed worthy of being kept.

She made no effort to budge. "Doing it my way saves you an extra step," she answered with a bright, broad, forced smile on her lips.

Just then, the door to 5F opened in response to Zane's knock. A slightly rumpled Harry McBride stood in the doorway wearing only pajama bottoms. He looked from the officer to her, an affable, slightly puzzled expression on his face. She'd never seen anyone appear so bemused and seemingly innocent before.

The man'd had practice, Alyx realized. Which made him diabolical.

"Hello." Harry nodded at Alyx, then looked back to the policeman. "Is there something I can help you with, Officer—?"

"Calloway," Zane told him, filling in the blank. "There's been a report of a domestic disturbance taking place in your apartment."

Harry seemed properly chagrined. "My fault," he admitted freely. "I've got a tendency to get a little carried away when I get excited about something I'm talking about. I don't realize how loud I can get sometimes." He deliberately looked at her and said with a sheepish, apologetic smile, "If I disturbed you, I am really sorry. I'll try not to let it happen again," he promised solemnly.

Alyx didn't believe him. Not for a moment. Didn't believe a word of Harry's charmingly recited explanation *or* his promise to her. He was just going through the motions to get rid of the policeman. She'd bet her life on it.

"Would you mind if we spoke to your wife?" Zane requested.

Harry hesitated, seemingly concerned. "Abby's had rather a hard day and she just now managed to drop off to sleep, but if you feel that it's necessary to talk to her, I can wake her up for you." With that, Harry turned on his heel, ready to go off to the bedroom and wake up his wife to accommodate the police.

Zane stopped the man before he went to his bedroom.

"No, that's all right. Let your wife sleep. Just remember to try to rein in your 'enthusiasm' next time," he cautioned the man. His business over, he saw no reason to put the other man out any further. "Have a good night, Mr. McBride. What's left of it," he added with a side glance toward Alyx.

With that, he turned away from the apartment.

"Good night," Harry echoed behind him, shutting the door.

"And that's it?" Alyx demanded, hissing the words at Calloway as the police officer began to walk away.

He stopped and deliberately pinned her with a less than charitable eye. "Unless you can think of something else."

It was clear by his tone that he didn't expect to be on the receiving end of any further input from her. His job here was done. He had a cold beer waiting for him in the refrigerator and he wanted to get to it.

"Unless I can think of something else?" Alyx echoed, staring at him in disbelief. "Yes, I can *think* of something else. How about talking to his wife? How about *looking* at his wife? One bruise one time means that she's being clumsy. More bruises means that she's someone's idea of a punching bag. Women like that need to be helped, to be guided. Because after a while, they start to think that they deserve it."

"Letting your imagination run away with you a little, aren't you?" Zane asked.

Still out in the hallway, he cocked his head to listen. "Well, it looks to me like the battling factions have decided to call it a night."

"They *weren't* battling factions," Alyx corrected tersely. "Battling factions would indicate that there were two sides. From the sound of it, Harry was the only one getting in his licks. All his wife was doing was whimpering pathetically like some wounded, frightened animal."

Another woman "crying wolf." She was wasting his time and he was tired. "Uh huh. Well, I don't hear anything now. Look at it this way, maybe you scared him into acting responsibly."

By the sarcasm in his voice, she knew the policeman didn't believe that—and neither did she. Harry McBride was a bully who would continue being a bully as long as he felt that no one would challenge him and he could get away with it.

About to leave, Zane hesitated for a moment. It was always good to cover your tail. His father had taught him that while he was still on the force, still part of his life. There were times when he couldn't help wondering how much more he would have been able to learn from his father had his father not cut his life so short.

Digging into his shirt pocket, Zane took out his business card. Handing it to the feisty, obviously dissatisfied blonde, he said purely for form sake, "If they start up again, call me."

Did that mean he finally believed her, or was he just humoring her in an effort to make a quick getaway with a clear conscience?

In either case, she intended on taking him up on what he'd just proposed.

Closing her fingers over the business card, Alyx raised her eyes to his. "I'll do that," she promised, her voice even.

Zane barely managed to suppress a world-weary sigh. "I'm sure that you will, Miss Pulaski."

"Doctor," Alyx corrected the cocky police officer. He raised a quizzical brow, so she elaborated, "It's Dr. Pulaski."

Zane inclined his head. "Sorry. *Dr.* Pulaski," he deliberately stretched out the name. "Good night now." And with that, he was on his way.

"Good night," Alyx echoed, calling after his retreating back. She walked into her apartment, trying her best to put the whole incident behind her.

She could more easily just stop breathing.

He didn't believe her, she thought, chewing on her lower lip as she closed her door. Officer Calloway didn't believe her. As an afterthought, she threw the dead bolt in place.

Why didn't he believe her?

What could she possibly have to gain by accusing Harry McBride of something he hadn't done? Only someone psychotic would do that.

With a shrug, Alyx tried to put the whole incident behind her again. She only had a few precious hours left before she had to turn up at the ER bright-eyed and bushy-tailed—and under the Dragon Lady's thumb.

God knew she needed her rest for that to happen. And rehashing the events of the past half hour over and over again simply would *not* give her that rest.

Alyx was halfway across the living room, on her way to the bedroom and her bed, when she heard the doorbell ring. She froze.

Had the officer forgotten something?

Or, better yet, had he changed his mind about why she'd made the call?

Hurrying back to the front door, Alyx threw it open before looking through the peephole, something she never did under ordinary circumstances. But anger and exhaustion had made her sloppy. And the need for validation had done the same.

Surprise throbbed through her veins.

She wasn't looking at the cynical officer with the sinful mouth. She was looking up at Harry McBride.

Gone like the pastel chalk marks of a brightly decorated sidewalk beneath the onslaught of a sudden, unexpected summer shower was the friendly, all-accommodating expression Harry had worn for the officer's benefit.

In its place was a cold, calculating look that could easily make a woman's blood all but contract within its veins.

The look in his eyes was positively malevolent. "Listen, I'm only going to say this once, hear? If you don't back off and mind your own damn business, I am going to make sure that you regret the day you ever moved into the building and started meddling in my life. Hell, I'm going to make you wish you were never born. Do I make myself clear?" he growled.

Mama, Alyx knew, would have insisted that she say she understood and then meekly withdraw out of the hulking ape's way. But she wasn't about to do as Mama said; she was about to do as Mama did. And that involved not allowing herself to be intimidated by a Neanderthal oaf. Ever.

She issued a threat of her own.

"If I see you lay another hand on Abby, *you* will be the one with regrets, Mr. McBride. I will report you so fast, your head will spin. And not just to some indifferent police officer. I have three cousins who are married to NYPD police detectives and they, I assure you, are no pushovers. You won't be able to snow them or lie your way out of the situation."

With each word Alyx uttered, she could see that Harry struggled more and more to keep from lashing out at her. The only thing, she felt certain, that kept him from hitting her was the fact that he didn't know whether or not she was telling him the truth about her relatives.

True cowards never tested boundaries—at least not when they could be easily identified. They fought dirty, with their identities hidden by masks or shadows. She would have to be extra careful for a while. And she would really need to watch her back.

"Go to hell!" McBride growled at her. The next

moment, he stomped back into his apartment and slammed the door so hard her own door shuttered in response.

Now there was someone definitely in need of anger management classes, Alyx mused, testing the integrity of her locks and the one chain that Marja's husband-to-be had put up for her at the insistence of all of her cousins. At the time she'd thought it was just so much overkill. After all, the building came with a doorman who didn't allow just anyone to saunter to the elevators. But now, she was glad that her cousins had overruled her protest and installed the chain.

Alyx glanced at her watch. Oh God. She now had only six more hours until her shift. She hurried off to the bedroom and prayed for a few hours of sleep.

Chapter 3

Unlike his partner, Zane Calloway, Officer Ryan Lukkas liked to talk. When he was nervous, he had a tendency to talk more. And faster. He was talking fast now. Very fast. And driving the exact same way.

"Dunno what this city's coming to, when two cops can't even walk into a convenience store in the middle of the day to get a couple of hot dogs and two cans of soda without some kind of a gun battle erupting," he complained loudly.

Officer Lukkas had raised his voice to compete with the blare of the siren that was piercing the usual ongoing din of the city. The siren was theirs and it was blaring for a very good reason. They needed to get to their destination. *Fast.*

Needed to, but so far it didn't look as if that was going to become a reality. Didn't people respond to sirens and flashing lights anymore? he silently demanded, cursing a blue streak in his head. Up to this point he'd managed to keep the words from erupting on his lips.

"Maybe it had something to do with you saying 'NYPD, drop your weapons,'" Zane suggested, his voice somewhat labored.

The careless shrug only involved one shoulder. "Yeah, maybe." He spared Zane a look, worried despite himself. "What else was I supposed to do?"

"Nothing else," Zane did his best to assure the man, though it got harder for him to focus. The pain was worsening. "You did the right thing."

C'mon, c'mon. Move! In addition to the siren, he blared his horn. Traffic slowed down even more. "You're only saying that so I don't feel guilty."

"I'm saying it," Zane replied in his dead, no-nonsense voice, "because it's true. You want to feel guilty about it, hell, that's up to you. Me, I'd say feeling guilty is a waste of time—and stupid—in this case anyway."

Ryan gave Zane another look and swallowed a curse, allowing the words "Oh damn" to break through. "How do you feel?" he pressed anxiously.

Zane's answer came out in a weakened growl. "Like I've been shot."

"Maybe I can drive on the sidewalk," he suggested as he looked at the area on either side of the street.

Today was particularly humid and miserable. Why couldn't these people stay at their jobs or in their homes?

It seemed as if every one of the eight million New York City inhabitants were out today, mostly milling around in the vicinity of the vehicle.

Lukkas blew out an impatient breath and slanted yet another look at Zane's arm. Of course, Zane knew it didn't look good. The towel that had been wrapped around it was heavy with blood.

"I want to be able to get to the hospital before you bleed to death," Ryan declared nervously.

"Anyone ever tell you that you're pretty lousy in the stay-calm department?" Zane asked him. "And I don't need to go to the hospital," he insisted, not for the first time. "Just stop at the closest pharmacy and get some bandages and gauze and peroxide." He looked down at his injured arm. "I can take care of this myself."

"Sorry, tough guy, you're outvoted. We both know that you'd be better off seeing a doctor."

"How the hell can I be outvoted?" Zane demanded sharply. "There's just the two of us."

"I've got two good arms to your one. That gives me two votes. Now shut up and save your strength."

"If I save my strength for anything," Zane warned him, "it'll be to strangle you."

"Fine," Ryan bit off, snaking the car around an ice cream truck that had its annoying theme song on. "First we get you patched up, then we'll discuss you strangling me. Fair enough?"

Zane inclined his head in agreement. There wasn't exactly much he could do, since Ryan was the one behind the wheel. Zane usually let his partner drive because traffic snarls and logjam conditions didn't seem to faze Ryan the way they did him.

"Fair enough," Zane echoed, repeating the phrase grudgingly.

Ryan definitely looked concerned, Zane thought. The man kept glancing at him as if his partner expected him to go up in smoke at any second. There was fear in Lukkas's eyes.

"I'm okay, Ryan," he assured the other officer. "I'd be more okay without a bullet in my arm, but I'm okay," he repeated. "Really," he underscored when his partner of a little more than a year made no answer. "There's no need to drive on the sidewalk. Look." He nodded toward the front windshield. "The cars are beginning to clear a path for us."

"About time," Ryan declared, mumbling under his breath. "We're the police—they should be clearing a path for us."

"The 'protect and serve' is in our part of the deal, not theirs," Zane reminded him. "They don't even have to be accommodating if they don't want to be—unless we arrest them."

Ordinarily, his partner wasn't this forgiving of the public. "You just want to argue," Ryan accused, flooring the vehicle, going all of fifteen yards before he had to slow down again.

Zane slowly let out a labored breath. Was it his imagination, or was it getting harder to breathe?

"No, I just want to stop bleeding. You could have stayed on the scene and brought the gunman in," Zane reminded him. There was no need for the man to do an imitation of a mother hen. "McKenzie could have taken me to the hospital. Hell, *I* could have taken me to the hospital."

"Number one, it was your shot that stopped the thief, so technically you should have been the one to take him in, not me. Two, McKenzie can't find his way out of a paper bag. It'd take him four hours to get to the 'nearest' hospital." He glanced toward his partner. "And you would have probably bullied him out of taking you there altogether. Aha, aha." One hand off the wheel, he pointed at Zane's face. "You're smiling."

"I'm grimacing, Lukkas," Zane corrected him. "You just drove over another damn pothole." This one had felt as if it was big enough to swallow the whole squad car— with room to spare. The jarring motion accentuated the pain in his arm.

"Sorry. Not my fault the city's falling apart faster than the mayor can come up with the money to fix it." The siren was on and the lights were flashing. Craning his neck, Ryan stuck his head out the window and shouted, "Get out of the way, damn it! Can't you hear the damn siren?" he shouted.

His words were all but swallowed up by the noise of the crowds as they made their way through the throngs of humanity that occupied the streets at any given moment of the day.

Zane stared straight ahead, trying to distract himself from the fire in his arm. The streets of the city were always crowded, but it seemed as if they were even more so at this particular time of the day. It was lunchtime.

He looked down at his arm, staring approximately where the bullet had gone in. He would have felt better if there was also an exit wound, but there wasn't. The bullet was still inside his arm, and despite the hastily secured "bandage" created out of the convenience store clerk's towel inventory, the wound was oozing blood. A lot of it.

And he was getting progressively more light-headed. Despite his efforts to concentrate, Zane could feel his grasp on his surroundings slipping away from him.

He didn't like not being in control, and he wasn't, not here.

Initially, Ryan had wanted to call for an ambulance, but waiting for one would have taken even longer, so he'd opted to allow his partner to drive him to the nearest hospital. In this case that was Patience Memorial.

He hoped that the name wasn't an indication of what he was going to need to have while he sat around, waiting to be seen.

"Hallelujah, we're here!" Ryan declared in much the same way that the Israelites must have sounded when, after forty years of aimless wandering, they finally reached the Promised Land.

Directly before the hospital's main entrance, a security guard directed traffic. Barely out of his teens, the guard stopped making exaggerated hand gestures as Ryan all but stopped right on top of him.

The security guard did his best to sound official.

"Emergency vehicle parking is to your left, Officer." The cheerful grin that punctuated his statement spoiled the effect.

"I've got a wounded officer here," Ryan announced gruffly, pulling the car into the first available space. "I'm bringing him in and then I'll be out to re-park."

Jumping out of the black and white, Ryan hurried around to the other side just as Zane opened his door. Zane felt as if the effort to do that simple thing had temporarily drained him. He struggled not to let his fatigue show. "I don't need you to hover around me, Lukkas."

"But you might need me to lean on," the shorter officer pointed out as Zane rose unsteadily to his feet, one hand braced against the hood of the vehicle.

The loss of blood had made him even more dizzy than he'd anticipated. A lot more. Zane scowled as he tried to support himself for a moment, leaning against the side of the vehicle. He didn't like displaying weakness of any kind. It was disconcerting enough to *be* weak, much less to show it. But apparently this wound left him no choice.

"Yeah, maybe," Zane finally said grudgingly.

Ryan raised his eyes to Zane's. There wasn't even a hint of a smile this time around. "Don't worry, I won't mention this later," Ryan promised.

Zane eyed him skeptically. Doubt was always his first emotion, but then he relented. "You're okay, Lukkas," he said quietly, staring straight ahead.

Ryan smiled, exceedingly pleased. "Coming from

you, that's like getting a five-star rating." With Zane's arm stretched across his stout shoulders and holding tightly on to the man's wrist while supporting his waist with his other hand, Ryan turned toward the security guard. "Which way's your ER?"

"You can get there right through here," the man said. His hand was already on the telephone receiver. "I can call for a wheelchair for you if—"

"You do and it's the last call you'll ever make," Zane growled. The security guard immediately stepped away from the wall unit.

"Can't take you anywhere," Ryan muttered, shaking his head.

"Nobody told you to," Zane reminded him with more than a little effort.

"Having a partner die on me would've looked bad on my record," Ryan informed him, a note of finality in his voice.

The ER was dead ahead, its entrance guarded by three registration booths, providing the first line of defense. A fast track was available for New York's finest, and the woman at the first desk immediately waved them into the interior of the facility. At the same time, she was on the intercom, alerting any available staff members that a wounded police officer was coming in and needed immediate attention.

In the middle of an outpatient procedure, Dr. Gloria Furst looked up in response to the announcement she'd just heard. She glanced around the area for the closest attending physician.

Her brown eyes narrowed as she found one.

"Pulaski," she called out. "Looks like you're up. See if you can help the man in blue without messing up this time."

Alyx's smile was one she'd practiced nightly in the mirror because glaring would only get her into more hot water. "I wasn't aware of messing up last time, doctor."

"I'm sure you weren't," the doctor commented crisply, her voice frosty. "But you'll learn, Pulaski. You'll learn—maybe."

Alyx drew in a deep breath, told herself that she could and *would* survive this nightmare and went to find her patient.

Her patient, she was told, was in trauma bed number seven. She made her way over to that section, which turned out to be closer to the front than the back.

Drawing back the curtain, Alyx didn't look at her newest patient until she was all but on top of him. And then she stopped dead.

Unwilling to lie down as the attending nurse had requested when she took his vitals, Zane was sitting up on the side of the bed. He came across as the very personification of impatience.

"You," he said in surprise when he saw her.

"Me," she confirmed. At least her breath was returning, she thought. Thank God for the small stuff. "Officer Calloway, I'd recognize that scowl anywhere," she added, infusing a deliberate note of cheerfulness into her voice. And then she looked at the wound. "Let me guess. Someone decide that they weren't thrilled with your attitude?"

"It was a convenience store robbery in progress. We stopped it," Ryan told her proudly, puffing up his barrel chest just a little. And then he smiled brightly. "Ryan Lukkas." Putting out his hand, he introduced himself. "I'm his partner."

"My condolences," Alyx replied, her face dead serious. After pulling on her umpteenth pair of rubber gloves, she gingerly removed the hastily applied, blood-soaked towel and then swiftly examined the wound. "Looks like you're carrying around some metal. The good news is, we can get it out without messing up an OR." She raised her eyes to his. "That is, if you're game. If not, I'll book an OR and we'll put you under."

He didn't want to waste any more time. Nodding at his arm, he said, "Do your worst."

She had a feeling that he only respected confidence. So she displayed it. "Have no fear, Officer. Even my 'worst' is damn good."

Stepping back, she called to a nearby nurse and requested a surgical extraction tray with a full complement of instruments, plus a local anesthetic and a needle and thread. The nurse returned quickly, bringing the tray and syringe with her. Setting everything down before Alyx, the older woman went to fetch the needle and thread.

Zane watched as she picked up the syringe. Although able to take a bullet—this wasn't his first—he'd never been very fond of needles. He blew out a breath, bracing himself. "You don't have to hang around," he told Ryan. "Go back to the precinct."

"You kidding?" Ryan cried. He had every intention of remaining to the bitter end. "I'm not about to leave you."

Zane didn't particularly want his partner hovering about, watching him trying not to wince. "Isn't he supposed to wait outside?" Zane asked Alyx.

"Not if he doesn't want to," she answered. She saw right through the man. "You afraid that you might show a little emotion, Officer Calloway?" she guessed.

He seemed to withdraw even further into himself right before her eyes. "Get on with it," he ordered.

The man would never run the risk of being voted Mr. Congeniality by his peers.

"Yes, sir," she retorted crisply as if she were a soldier and he the high-ranking commanding officer. "This won't take too long," she assured him. "We'll be done before you know it."

Alyx unwrapped the tray and left it positioned on a small, adjustable hospital table. Reaching for a small, rectangular packet, she tore it open and removed the antiseptic wipe from inside. Unfolding it, she liberally applied the wipe to his wound, making sure she got the entire area and beyond. The officer stiffened as if he'd been shot again. The antiseptic packed quite a sting.

Heaven forgive her, she felt a fleeting surge of satisfaction.

"Hurt?" she asked.

"No."

Alyx was fairly certain that Officer Calloway would deny feeling any pain even if he had a bayonet sticking into him. Her father had been that kind of a man, refusing to acknowledge pain because real men didn't complain.

Gritting his teeth, trying to think of other things, Zane allowed his eyes to slide over her scrubs. "So I guess you really are a doctor."

She widened her tolerant smile. The man was not the smoothest talker. Finished, she tossed the wipe into a wastebasket. "Yup. Got my diploma from the back of a comic book and everything."

"Sorry. Didn't mean to insult you."

"You didn't." She spread out the instruments on the tray, wanting to make sure she had everything she needed before she got started. "But you did rub me the wrong way the other night."

"You rubbed her?" Ryan blurted out, his eyes wide. He'd been silently listening all this time, trying not to get on Zane's nerves. The bullet in his partner's arm had been meant for him. If Zane hadn't pushed him aside, he'd be the one on the hospital bed now—or a slab in the morgue. "And you didn't say anything? Damn it, Zane, you've really gotta learn how to share and tell me things. I'm your partner."

Zane fixed him with a cold look. "That can be changed."

Alyx glanced at Calloway's partner, who came across a great deal more affable than the man she was about to work on. "So I take it that he's this surly with everyone?" she asked the officer.

Ryan nodded and allowed a sigh to escape. "For the most part."

"Again, my condolences," she said. Reaching for the syringe, she held it up and pressed the plunger just enough to release the tiniest drop of solution to make sure that there wasn't an air bubble going into his arm. "This'll numb your arm so that you won't feel anything while I'm working," she explained.

"Too late," he bit off, his arm still stung from the antiseptic she'd applied.

For some reason, he could almost feel her smile across his lips as it slid over hers. "Then I guess in this situation we can say better late than never," she countered.

Alyx paused just before she gave him the injection, pretending that she was trying to recall the steps to the procedure.

"Now, how much of this do I give you?" she murmured under her breath.

"You don't know?" Zane exclaimed, suddenly alert.

The next second, Alyx jabbed the needle just above his wound.

"It just came back to me," she informed him cheerfully, then did it again, this time injecting him just below the wound.

Zane gritted his teeth and stared straight ahead. He could feel moisture gathering in his eyes. Damn it, now she would think he was crying.

In all honesty, Zane couldn't remember the last time he had cried. Maybe never. He hadn't even cried at his father's funeral.

The day his heart officially broke.

Chapter 4

The ER doctor was right, Zane thought. His arm had gone numb. Completely and utterly numb. He was vaguely aware of having an appendage, but that was it. He was nervous.

"This is just temporary, right?" Zane asked the woman working over him. "The feeling in my arm, it's going to come back, right?"

Alyx raised her eyes to his for a split second and was surprised to detect a glimmer of anxiety in the deep blue orbs. He didn't strike her as the type to be anxious about anything.

"All too soon," she assured him, resuming what she was doing. "You're going to need a prescription for painkillers. I'll write it up for you once I get this bullet out and get you all sewn up."

"Dunno about his needing painkillers," Ryan interjected. He stood leaning against the back wall, his arms crossed before his chest, an all but silent witness to the procedure. "Calloway bends steel in his bare hands."

This was not the time to try to talk him up, Zane thought. "Shut up, Lukkas," he muttered.

Her eyes, he noticed, were laughing as she raised them to his. He also noticed that they were a brilliant shade of blue. The kind of blue that stayed with you after you walked away.

"No bending steel for at least a week," she instructed.

He knew she was kidding, but there was a note of restriction in her voice. Restrictions always made him chafe. "But I'll still be cleared to go back to work, right?"

"That all depends." She stopped for a moment to look at him. "Does 'work' mean sitting behind a desk?"

"Only if they duct taped him to a chair," Ryan volunteered with a laugh. "And even then it would be touch and go."

Zane really didn't need Ryan's "helpful" comments. Nor did he want a witness to his having the bullet dug out of the fleshy part of his shoulder.

"Why don't you get back to the precinct, Lukkas?" Zane suggested again, this time more forcefully. "The captain's probably looking for you."

It was getting late and Ryan knew he'd feel better making his own report to the captain. McKenzie was an annoying glory hound and he liked nothing better than taking credit for something positive—even if it didn't belong to him.

Still, there was a loose end to consider. "What are you going to use for transportation?" Ryan asked Zane.

Transportation was the last thing on his mind right now. "When the time comes, I'll improvise," Zane answered. "Maybe I'll even give you a call," he added, knowing that was what the other man was hoping to hear. For some reason, to Lukkas that would mean that they were bonding.

But rather than take off, Ryan hesitated. He slanted a look in the doctor's direction to see if she gave her blessings to his departure.

Zane caught the small, almost imperceptible nod she gave his partner. And felt the more positive attitude that Lukkas assumed.

"Okay, then," Ryan declared. "I'm off. But you call me the second the doctor's done patching you up and they let you leave here, understand?" Ryan instructed.

Zane said nothing. Instead, his partner gave him a penetrating look. Ryan realized that he had overstepped his boundaries. He'd dictated rather than merely put the suggestion out there. Zane didn't appreciate being dictated to.

Changing his tone, Ryan asked brightly, "Okay?"

It cost him nothing to be agreeable, even if he didn't mean it. "Okay," Zane replied.

Ryan blew out a breath, suddenly looking as if he was at loose ends. "Okay then," he murmured, flashed an unsteady grin at the sexy surgeon and ambled out of the small area.

The man had muscles like a rock, Alyx thought, slowly probing around the wound for the bullet that had caused it.

"You like intimidating him?" she asked mildly.

"I'm not intimidating him," Zane contradicted. "Just not letting him act as if he's in charge."

Again he saw that smile, the one he found unnervingly seductive. There was also amusement. "Because you are."

Was she mocking him? Or just trying to bait him? He couldn't tell.

"I have seniority," Zane said, neither agreeing or disagreeing with her assumption.

Amusement curved her mouth and he decided that she had a nice smile. A *really* nice smile. Something vaguely familiar stirred within him, but he couldn't quite put his finger on what it was. These days, his work took up all his available time. When he wasn't working, he was usually asleep. It kept him from thinking, or remembering.

Or noticing the emptiness in his belly that had nothing to do with food.

"Which makes you in charge," Alyx concluded.

This would go faster if the man had slacked off and skipped a few workouts. She held her breath as she continued probing, waiting until she heard the sound of metal on metal: her scalpel hitting the bullet. And then there it was, the point of her scalpel touching the lethal part of the bullet. They were in business.

"Okay, we're almost past the worst part," she told him. He was being very quiet. She didn't even hear him breathing. Sparing him a glance as she worked the bullet out of his flesh, she asked, "How are you doing?"

He watched her work in utter fascination. "Don't feel a thing."

She detected a note of frustration in his voice. He had no idea how lucky he was not to "feel a thing." "Good."

But it wasn't, he thought. Not feeling anything made you hollow and that was how he felt, *had* felt for a lot of years. As if he was hollow. Unable to reach out, unable to forge any sort of a relationship with a woman. He had nothing to draw on as an example. All he remembered was shouting. Words of recrimination would bounce back and forth between his parents with frightening regularity. No words of endearment counterbalanced that, no warmth at all, other than the type that came from a heater in the garage.

"If you say so," Zane commented on the doctor's pronouncement.

Finally coaxing her quarry out into the open, Alyx deposited the bullet into the corner of the tray with no small feeling of triumph.

She glanced at her patient. His expression was completely neutral. He neither looked happy to be done with it or grimacing in anticipation of the pain.

"You are a very complex human being, Officer Calloway," she commented.

He said nothing.

Alyx began to clean the wound again, making it as sterile as possible before she started sewing up the hole. The ensuing silence made her uncomfortable.

"So, are you a Yankees fan, or do you like to root for the underdog and cheer for the Mets?" she asked him as she prepared the sutures and needle.

Zane lifted his other shoulder and let it drop dismissively. He'd never watched more than a part of a game and those instances only occurred when he was at someone else's place and they were watching the event. He had no use for watching grown men swinging a stick at a ball.

"Neither."

There was finality in his voice. She raised an eyebrow in his direction. "You don't follow baseball?" she concluded.

Zane moved his head from side to side only once. "No."

She tried to remember if she'd ever met anyone who didn't root for their home team. "How about football?"

The answer was the same. "No."

"Basketball?" she guessed. "Soccer?"

"No and no."

She wasn't about to give up. There had to be some sport he enjoyed watching if not playing. He didn't make her think of someone who liked being on the sidelines. "Bowling? The poker channel?"

Each question drew out the same answer. His "no" grew a little firmer each time.

He completely fascinated her. "A man not into sports. I didn't know there was such a creature." Her smile raced straight into his insides, pureeing them before he could think to sideline it. "Maybe you're not so complex after all."

His reasons sounded completely plausible to him. "I don't have time to follow sports."

What did he do that fired his imagination so much it kept him away from vegging out before his set at least once a week? she wondered. "What do you have time for?"

He tossed the word at her carelessly. "Work."

"I bet that goes over big with your wife."

Zane made an unintelligible noise. Then, because she continued to look at him as if waiting for an answer, he said, "I'm not married."

"Divorced?" she guessed. That was what half the people she knew were. "Widowed?" she tossed in for good measure when he made no answer.

"Does any of this have any kind of bearing on you getting the bullet out of my arm?"

"No," she answered simply. "But it makes the time go by that much faster." She punctuated her statement by slipping the needle beneath his skin and taking another stitch.

That one pinched a little. Or maybe it was his

imagination. He tried to think of something else. "Your neighbors giving you any more trouble?" he asked before she could fire off another round of questions he had no intentions of answering.

"They weren't giving me trouble in the first place," Alyx countered. "I called 911 because I was afraid that Harry was beating his wife. There was a lot of yelling and things crashing. I was worried about Abby's safety."

In other words, he thought cynically, the doctor used that as an excuse to butt in. "Have you heard them fighting lately?"

"No, as a matter of fact, I haven't." She didn't know if that was a good thing or just the calm before another storm. She completely distrusted Abby's husband. "I guess you must have the magic touch," she said. Finished, she knotted her surgical thread and then cut it off.

Not a bad job, Alyx, even if I do have to say so myself.

"Okay," she told him, packing up the tray, "you're all done." She smiled at him, her eyes sweeping over the police officer. "You can go back to being the city's Dark Knight."

He frowned at her words. "That's a fictional character."

"Then it won't be that hard to take his place," she informed him cheerfully, stripping off her gloves and dropping them into the trash can. She'd already tucked away the syringe into the hazardous waste container with its one-way-only slot. All that was left to do was to write out his prescriptions. "You should like that."

"I don't mind competition." His eyes swept over her slowly. So slowly that she could *feel* the touch of his gaze. Feel it warming her from the outside in. "I'd like to buy you a cup of coffee to say thanks, Doc. When's your next break?"

Okay, so this man utterly defied being pegged. The invitation for coffee was the very *last* thing she would have expected from him. She had him down as being a loner. Loners didn't offer to buy a woman a cup of coffee. Even if she *had* taken a bullet out of his shoulder.

"Oddly enough, now," she told him. "But it's not a long break."

"Wasn't planning on going to Paris for it. Just to the hospital cafeteria."

She realized that she was nodding her head before responding. She supposed there was nothing wrong in having a cup of coffee together. She'd rather make a friend out of him than think of him as "that surly policeman."

"All right," she agreed. "Just let me get your discharge papers together along with a list of instructions."

"Instructions?" he repeated quizzically.

She nodded. "On how to take care of your wound once you leave here."

"This isn't the first time I've been shot," he told her. "I know what to do."

Good for you. The man was cocky, no doubt about it. "First order of business is not to get shot again."

He wasn't aware of the corners of his mouth curving, but she was. "Don't remember that being on the list the last ER doctor gave me."

He didn't look nearly as forbidding with that half-smile, she thought. "It's my own personal touch," she told him.

His eyes seemed to pin her in place—and then strip her down to the bare flesh. "You like being unique?"

Had someone suddenly turned up the heat in here? Alyx wondered. Because she could have sworn the temperature had gone up by a good ten degrees. She struggled to keep any of this from showing on her face.

"Never knew any other way," Alyx quipped. Gathering up the tray she'd just used, she pulled open the curtain on her side. "Stay put. I'll be back with your discharge papers in a couple of minutes."

He nodded in response.

True to her word, Alyx was back in a couple of minutes.

Untrue to his, he wasn't there.

When Alyx returned, Zane was nowhere to be seen. Surprised—the coffee had been his idea, not hers—she stared at the empty bed for a moment, as if she expected him to somehow just reappear. And then she turned around and stopped an orderly who was passing by.

"Did you see the man who was in this bed?" she asked. "He's a police officer and he was supposed to wait for his discharge papers."

"Sorry, doctor, I didn't notice anyone here. I'm

working on the other side of the ER today. I just came over to see if you have any extra sheets over here. We've run out." With that, he went to look in the closet where the sheets and extra blankets for this side of the ER were kept.

Where the hell had Calloway gone?

"Um, doctor?" the man in the next bed began hesitantly, raising his hand to get her attention just as if he were in a classroom.

She looked in his direction. "Yes?"

"The man in this bed? The guy you're looking for? He got a call on his cell phone. Didn't hear what he said except for, 'Damn it, I'll be right there,' and then he just got up and left. Real quick like."

Who was that masked man? Alyx thought, mocking herself.

Most likely, it was better this way. She had a feeling that even going out for coffee with Office Calloway was just another way of asking for trouble. Heaven knew she didn't have time for any extra trouble. She had enough with unkindly Dr. Gloria riding her as if she was a year-old filly that needed breaking.

With an appreciative smile, she nodded at the man in the bed. "Thank you for filling me in."

Picking up the chart that was hanging off the end of the man's bed, she scanned the nurse's notes quickly to familiarize herself with his condition.

"So, tell me, Mr…" She glanced down at the third line for his name. "Fontaine, what brings you here to us today?"

A widower with an eye for the ladies, Mr. Fontaine was only too glad to tell her. Slowly.

Her feet were killing her.

Alyx felt like she'd been standing on them for the past three days without a break. She couldn't even remember the last time she'd sat down. Right after Calloway disappeared, the ER had turned into nonstop craziness.

Lunch was tabled when three ambulances arrived simultaneously, bringing in the victims of a tour-bus-meeting-a-semi accident. According to the report taken by the first officer on the scene, the tour bus driver had turned back to look at his passengers for a split second as he was doing his regular round of banter-laced information.

It was the wrong split second.

There'd been no letup after that. The only good thing was that tonight she wasn't being asked to take up any slack or to fill in for anyone who had neglected to come in. Tonight everyone who was supposed to be here, was here.

Alyx smiled to herself as she changed into her street clothes. Tonight she might even feel human.

"So how's it going, Alyx?"

For a moment she didn't recognize the voice. Turning around, Alyx saw the youngest of her five cousins, Marja, peering into the locker room. Wearing her street clothes, Marja was obviously headed out.

There was no lack of caring or warmth about her

cousins. Mama had been *so* wrong about them. About her uncle and aunt as well. "When does it get easier?"

Marja laughed. "Sorry to have to tell you this, but it doesn't. But I can also tell you that eventually you start to realize that you *do* know what you're doing and you won't wind up killing your patients—although there will be some you wish you could. Is there anything I can do for you before I head out?" Marja asked.

"Yes," Alyx responded with feeling. "Teach me how to do without sleep."

Marja shook her head. "No can do. If you find out, let me know. Please." About to leave, she remembered why she'd sought Alyx out in the first place. "Almost forgot. I'm here to relay a message," she told her cousin. "Mama told me to invite you over to the house for dinner this Sunday. Three o'clock. Bring your appetite. Maybe don't eat for two days," she suggested. "The more you eat, the happier Mama is."

This invitation felt different than the rest. "Anything important?"

"Yes. Dinner. Mama takes cooking very seriously," Marja told her, not bothering to hide her broad smile. "Oh, and there's something else."

Marja jerked a thumb toward the entrance. "There's a cop waiting outside. He says he's here to see you. You do something to run afoul of New York's finest?" she asked, only half teasing.

Alyx shook her head. "Not that I know of."

"Well, if you do, just give Natalya a call. She'll send Mike—or call Sasha, who'll get Tony to handle things for you. Now that you're here and part of us, you've got an in with the NYPD," she told her with a wink.

Alyx smiled. "Nice to know." She paused for a moment, searching for the right words. "Marja?"

Already on her way out, her cousin turned around to look at her. "Yes?"

"I just wanted to tell you how grateful I am to you—to all of you. It's been kind of a rough year, and it's just nice to know that there's someone I can turn to for advice or just to hang out with."

Marja crossed back to the lockers and gave her a quick, warm hug. "Honey, we've always been here. All you had to do was call out."

Alyx nodded, somewhat embarrassed. "My mother had some things to work out."

Marja dismissed it with an understanding laugh. "Don't we all? What counts is that you're here—and coming to dinner on Sunday."

"I'll be there," Alyx promised.

Marja nodded and started for the door again. "Oh, and don't forget about that policeman waiting in the hallway."

Alyx closed her locker and gave the combination lock a quick twist. "On my way to see him right now," she told her cousin. Her curiosity was definitely aroused. It couldn't be who she thought it was.

Could it?

Chapter 5

Zane shifted his weight and debated leaving. He hadn't been waiting long, but he wasn't sure why he was here in the first place.

Maybe his sense of order required him to come back to the hospital and offer some excuse to the woman who had patched him up. She had to be wondering why he'd pulled a disappearing act. Taking off wasn't all that bad in his opinion, except that he *had* extended an invitation to her to grab a cup of coffee.

He didn't feel accountable to anyone but himself and this wasn't the sort of behavior he condoned—despite the fact that he'd had a good reason. She had no way of knowing that unless he told her.

So he'd asked one of the detectives he knew, Mike

diPalma, about shift changes at the hospital. He'd heard that diPalma was married to a doctor who had surgical privileges at Patience Memorial. diPalma hadn't known the exact time when the day shift ended, but he put in a call to his mother-in-law, a woman who was, according to diPalma, a walking encyclopedia about her daughters.

Which was how he had come to be standing in the hall next to the entrance to the doctors' locker room at this particular time. When the door opened, as it had several times already since he'd stationed himself here, he watched with hooded eyes to see who came out of the locker room.

What the hell are you doing here?

The question echoed in his head as his envoy emerged from the lockers.

You're taking things too far, he mocked himself. *You don't need to make up for before.*

The ER doc had probably forgotten all about the incident by now. He couldn't have been the first patient to skip out on her before the final discharge orders were issued. This was New York, a city composed of eight million independent thinkers who, at times, marched to eight million different drummers.

The door to the lockers opened again. This time, it was the ER doc.

Zane instantly straightened, his back severing contact with the wall he'd been leaning against.

"So it is you," Alyx said, a bit surprised that Calloway was here, although for the life of her, she couldn't come up with a single reason any other policeman would have been out here, waiting to see her. "Is something wrong? Do you feel weak, or—"

"I'm fine," he assured her. "Won't be arm wrestling for a while, but otherwise, I'm okay."

"Then what are you doing here?"

"I promised you a cup of coffee," he said simply.

She stared at him. If this had come from another man, she would have said he was coming on to her. She found it difficult to reconcile that image with the man who stood before her. "This is a little out of character, don't you think?"

He never liked being read or analyzed. He considered it an invasion of his privacy. "Doc, with all due respect, you don't know what my character is."

Alyx studied him for a long moment before rendering a contradiction.

"Loner to a fault, given to one-word sentences whenever possible. Feels accountable to no one but himself. Has a strict moral code he doesn't talk about. Would swerve to avoid hitting an animal—and possibly an adult—but definitely a child. Feels it's okay to bend the rules as long as he's the one doing the bending. How am I doing?" He grunted and she smiled. The flicker in his eyes told her that she'd hit the nail on the head—repeatedly. "You're not as mysterious as you'd like to think. What really brought you back?"

"My sense of duty," he told her simply. He didn't like explaining himself, but he had been the one to open the door to this so he couldn't very well blame her for asking questions. "I didn't want to leave you stuck with those discharge papers. And, like I said, I did promise you a cup of coffee."

She wasn't entirely sure if he was on the level or not. "I would have found a way to survive. In both cases. I still have those papers. They're in a folder on the nurse's desk in the ER. If you're serious about tying up loose ends, come with me and I'll get them for you."

He gestured for her to go first. "Lead the way."

The ER was located only one corridor down from the locker room. Getting the papers took less than five minutes. When he signed them, she handed off the discharge papers to a nurse, who dutifully took them to be filed away.

Alyx turned to face the patrolman. "There, your conscience is clear."

This was where he should take his cue and leave. Because something in the woman's eyes warned him he might regret taking the road ahead.

Something else told him he might regret not taking it.

"Not quite," he answered. Zane held the door that led out of the ER open for her, then followed her out. "And it's not a matter of conscience, it's a matter of doing what I said I would do. I still owe you a coffee."

As tempted as she was—because the man was very compelling—she knew trouble when she saw it. And Zane Calloway was big trouble. Right now, she needed to concentrate on her profession.

"I absolve you of your debt. Consider it paid. I'm sure you have better places to be than a hospital cafeteria."

The only other place right now was home. An apartment where his memories waited in the shadows to haunt him. It could keep.

"Like I said, you know nothing about me. I think you'd be better off not making any assumptions. And it doesn't have to be coffee from the cafeteria." He'd heard it was only a grade above used dishwater. "There's a deli about a block away. Lukkas told me that they make a pretty decent cup of coffee there." He realized she might not know who he was referring to. "Lukkas is—"

Alyx nodded, cutting in. "Your partner, yes, I know. I was paying attention this afternoon. Nice man. He worries about you," she informed him in case Calloway had missed that. "Well, if Officer Lukkas recommends it, then I guess we owe it to him to check the place out." But she wasn't going to feel right about the venture until she added a caveat. "As long as you don't feel obligated to take me."

He was impatient to get going and was leading the way out. "Do you argue all the time?"

Calloway's take on what she'd just said surprised her. "That wasn't arguing—that was just making my position clear. Trust me, you'll know when I'm arguing." God but he had a long stride. She practically had to skip to keep up with him—but she refused to tell him to slow down for her. "Arguing involves anger. I have no reason to be angry with you."

His mouth seemed to curve on its own. He thought

of something that Billy, his youngest brother, had once said. That he could make a saint angry. "Give it time."

"Why? How many people are angry with you?"

Reaching the front entrance, he pushed open the door for her, stretching to allow her to go first. "I don't keep a tally. Some days, it feels like everyone."

The man had impressive manners. She liked that. Alyx laughed in response to what he'd just said.

"I think that has something to do with living in New York City. Everyone here's always rushing. Constantly," she pronounced. "If you don't feel as if you're getting somewhere fast enough, you get angry."

"You're not from around here, then?"

"Initially, yes. But my mother uprooted the family and moved to Chicago when my father was killed."

Chicago wouldn't have been his first choice in fleeing New York. It seemed like too much of a leaping from the frying pan into the fire kind of thing. He would have thought that the idea behind transplanting a family would involve going somewhere a little more slow-paced and suburban.

"Mugging?" he guessed, thinking of the convenience store clerk.

"Not exactly. My father fell on the subway tracks just as a train was coming into the station. The police ruled it an accident."

"But you didn't."

"I was too young to rule it anything. But my mother thought he was pushed. She blamed my uncle for my father's death and couldn't get us away fast enough."

He looked at her, confused. "She thought your uncle pushed your father onto the tracks?"

"No, but my uncle was the reason we were all here in New York. If we hadn't been here, there wouldn't have been a subway to fall in front of, etcetera."

"Chicago has a subway system," he pointed out.

She flashed a smile and he watched a dimple wink in and out of the corner of her mouth. "Ironic, isn't it? I didn't say that my mother made perfect sense. She reacted emotionally."

"Like a woman."

"Like a person who lost someone they loved deeply."

"How young was 'too young'?" he asked.

"Excuse me?"

"You said you were too young to have an opinion about whether or not your father's death was an accident or a homicide. How old were you when your father died?" he wanted to know.

"Eight."

He nodded, and she thought she glimpsed a momentary faraway look in his eyes. "Still old enough to leave an impression."

"Was that how old you were?"

"How old I was when what?"

"When your father died."

He started to protest that this wasn't supposed to be an exchange of information. He was far more accustomed to gathering information than to giving any out. But the fact that this perky woman had figured that out all on her own did rather fascinate him. "I was ten."

"I'm sorry."

He shrugged. That part of him had been sealed off and he wasn't about to open the door, not even a crack. "It happens."

"How did it happen?" Alyx asked.

"Abruptly," was all he was willing to say. Pointing straight ahead, he said, "There's the shop Lukkas mentioned." Since it was approaching evening, he felt he should expand the invitation. "Would you like something to eat?"

She shook her head. "Just coffee'll be fine. I don't want to keep you from anything."

"You're not," he told her, his voice even, mild. "If I needed to be somewhere else, I would be."

"So I'm a last resort to stave off boredom?" she asked, amused.

"That's not what I meant. How long have you been back in New York?" When he saw her glance at her wristwatch, he made the only logical connection. "You keep track of it in hours?"

"No," she laughed, "I have a calendar on my watch. Sometimes, with these extra shifts they keep piling on, I tend to lose track of the days. I've been in the city for six weeks."

He was here because he was here, and it was easier to remain than to go. But if he had been transplanted, there was no way he would have returned. "What brought you back?"

She paused for a moment as it came back to her. The pride that filled her when she opened her acceptance letter. And the cloud that instantly descended when she broke the news to her mother. Paulina Pulaski had just assumed that all her daughters would remain somewhere within the state. Her dreams for all of them had their limitations. "I was accepted by Patience Memorial to complete my residency."

As good a reason as any, he supposed. The women he interacted with had a street savvy to them that this one seemed to be lacking. There was an innocence to her that didn't belong here. She was better suited to white picket fences and a slower pace.

"Miss home?" he asked, thinking he knew the answer.

But he was wrong.

"Actually, most of home is going to be coming out here," she told him. When he continued watching her, obviously waiting for an explanation, she elaborated. "My sisters just graduated from medical school last spring, or at least two of them did. They'll be coming to New York to do their residency at Patience Memorial, too." She smiled as she thought about having them all out here. It'll be like old times—except without the hair pulling. "My cousins pulled a few strings. They're all doctors at Patience Memorial. The place will be overflowing with Pulaskis."

Her father would have liked that, she couldn't help thinking. There were times when he was a mere shadow, a man whose face she could no longer remember clearly. At other times, memories would bust over her, brought on by a sound or a smell, and those times his image was so vivid it was as if he was in the next room.

"It's a great hospital," Alyx added enthusiastically.

Zane nodded. "So I hear."

They gave their order to the tired-looking teenager behind the counter and waited. She wanted a mocha latte. He'd ordered a coffee, black—exactly what she would have guessed that he'd get.

When their order was filled, they took a table near the door.

"Where did you go?" Alyx asked abruptly as she sat down.

Zane looked at her quizzically. He hadn't gone anywhere. He'd been beside her the entire time. "Come again?"

"This afternoon, when I went to get your discharge papers, you disappeared suddenly. Where did you go?" she repeated, then took a guess. "Did you get a call from the precinct?"

"No." He was going to leave it at that. There was no point in telling her that his brother Billy had called, despondent and high, talking about doing away with himself. But she was obviously waiting for him to continue. "I got a call from someone I knew. They needed help." All of which was true, he thought. Just vague.

"Girlfriend?" she asked.

He looked at her sharply, expecting to find a coy expression on her face. There was nothing but innocence in her eyes. She was simply asking after the identity of his caller.

"If that were the case, I wouldn't be sharing a cup of coffee with you. No girlfriend. We covered that earlier," he reminded her.

She turned what he'd just said over in her head. Had he extended the invitation for coffee to her because she was a woman, or because he'd been rude earlier?

"So if I were a male physician and had treated you, we wouldn't be sitting here in this shop, having coffee?" she asked.

He preferred just letting things be, not having them analyzed. "It's a little more complicated than that," he finally said.

She took a sip of her latte and let the warm liquid wind its way through her system. "I'm off duty, I've got time. Enlighten me."

He had no intention of turning this into some long-winded story. He gave her the highlights. "Short as it is, we did have a history before Lukkas dragged me into the ER. I might have been rather rude that other night—"

"You were," she interjected.

He chose to ignore her comment and push on. "You didn't try to even the score today, so I figured I owed you."

"Even the score," she repeated, a little mystified. Just what kind of people was this man used to? "Did you expect me to extract the bullet from your arm using pliers?"

Obviously amused by her question, for the first time

since she'd met him, Zane grinned. It transformed his face from forbidding to sunny.

For a moment, it quite literally took her breath away.

One shoulder moved in a semi-shrug. Zane addressed his coffee cup with the answer. "Maybe something like that."

"If that's the case, then letting you buy me a cup of coffee—"

He nodded at the cup. "Mocha latte."

She kept on going as if she hadn't heard him. "—is really letting you off the hook cheap."

"Hey, I did ask you if you wanted something to eat," he reminded her. "I can still snag a menu for you if you're serious."

Lunch had been a granola bar. The thought of food right now was tempting, but she didn't want to be indebted to him. Paying her own way always made things easier for her—which was why she was having a hard time accepting her cousins' generosity. Somehow, she would find a way to repay them, or die trying.

"I'll settle for an answer," she told him.

Zane looked at her skeptically. He was not one to tacitly agree to something without knowing its boundaries. A man could get into a whole lot of trouble that way. "To what?"

"To who called you in the ER."

This was really bothering her, he thought and wondered why. "What does it matter?"

"It doesn't in the grand scheme of things, but I'm

curious. It's a curse," she freely admitted. "I always read the last chapter of a book first before I make up my mind to buy it."

"I take it that you don't like surprises," he assumed.

"I don't like being unprepared," she corrected, deliberately keeping her voice mild.

It had taken Alyx years to figure out that her feelings were rooted to that awful, awful morning when her world had been shattered. The morning that her Uncle Josef had come to tell her mother that Papa wouldn't be coming home that night because he was dead. That gentle, gentle man with the powerful hands and deep, resonant voice, the man who provided the stability of her world and made her feel as if nothing would ever harm her as long as he was there, was gone.

Just like that.

She might have only been eight, but the feeling of being utterly lost and abandoned had gone deep down to her bones. It had taken a very long time for her to get over that.

In his experience, most women liked spontaneity. "There's something to be said for surprises."

"Yes, there is," Alyx agreed, remembering. "And it's all bad."

He had to admit, she intrigued him. "Let me guess. You were the one who opened all her Christmas presents ahead of time."

Mama and she and her sisters had gone through some very lean times in the years that followed their exodus from New York. *Food first, gifts later,* her mother, a pillar of practicality, had said.

"When there were any," Alyx said, brushing the subject aside. "Now stop changing the subject. Who called you?"

"It was just my brother," he told her mildly. "No big deal."

But it was a big deal, she thought. Big enough to make him rush out rather than wait to make his excuses or take a rain check. And then there was the matter of his wording. "You said he needed you."

What he should have done, Zane thought, was lied. He should have said yes when she'd guessed that the call had come in from his precinct. Being honest could create more hassles than it smoothed out.

"He's a little clueless and tends to get confused easily."

She would bet a month's salary that there was more to this, but she knew what it felt like to be probed, to be made to feel that she was under a microscope, so she left it alone. Even though her curiosity was far from satisfied.

"Maybe I will have that sandwich," she said, opening up the menu.

Zane merely nodded, relieved that she had decided to stop asking questions—but he couldn't help wondering how long that would last.

Chapter 6

Rather than say goodbye at the sandwich shop, Zane offered to drive her home. Because her car was in the shop, she was grateful for the offer.

Parking in a space reserved strictly for emergency vehicles, Zane got out and walked her to the front door of the building, expecting to hand Alyx off to the doorman.

Except that there was no doorman at the entrance.

"Your doorman take off somewhere?" Zane asked as he looked through the double glass doors into the foyer. The doorman wasn't at his post inside the building either.

The fact that there was a doorman, Alyx knew, had been an important selling feature for both her aunt and her uncle. The two worried a great deal about their daughters' safety in the city. Especially her uncle, who was a retired policeman and knew firsthand about the darker side of life on the streets.

Glancing at her watch, Alyx made a calculated guess. "Most likely, he's probably just on a break."

If that was the case, he might as well do it the right way, Zane decided. After all, he was a cop and "protect and serve" was part of the creed. "Then maybe I should ride up the elevator with you and take you to your door myself." He was thinking out loud. There was no "maybe." Taking her to her door was what he intended to do.

Despite her mother's tendency to hover—or maybe because of it—Alyx had been extremely and stubbornly independent ever since she could remember. It was on the tip of her tongue to say that she'd managed this "tricky" transition from the ground floor to her apartment door on her own for the last month and a half and there was no reason to believe that she had suddenly lost that "unique" ability.

But the idea of having someone seeing her home, especially when that someone was as good-looking as Zane Calloway, was not exactly a displeasing thought. So rather than turn him down, she murmured, "That would be nice," and led the way into the building.

The elevator door opened almost immediately after he'd pressed for it. They had the car all to themselves the entire trip up to the fifth floor.

It had to be her imagination, but the elevator had

never felt quite as small to her as it did at this moment. She couldn't quite explain it, but she was in Zane's space and he in hers.

She knew that he was also aware of it. All she had to do was look into his eyes to know.

The air crackled between them, just as it had when she'd sewn up his wound. She'd treated other men before, had sewn up a four-inch gash on a muscular thirty-something dock worker just a couple of weeks ago, but this was different. There hadn't been this charge of electricity rushing through her when she'd tended to the dock worker. And, on an absolute scale, the dock worker had been a more flawlessly attractive specimen of manhood than the police officer next to her.

And yet...

And yet she was making no sense, Alyx silently upbraided herself. Her thoughts were hazy. Most likely she was just a victim of static electricity, nothing more.

The elevator doors opened and she walked to her apartment quickly.

"Suddenly remember that you left something on the stove?" Zane asked mildly, lengthening his stride to keep up with her.

She glanced over her shoulder at him just before she reached her door. "What? No. Why?"

"Because you're almost sprinting to get to the door," he pointed out, "and I don't remember anyone yelling out, 'Tag, you're it.'"

"I'm not sprinting," she informed him, embarrassed

as she reached the door. She rummaged through her purse for her keys. Although her purse was small, it took her several seconds to locate the elusive key ring. "I was just moving fast so that you can get back to your own schedule." She produced the key ring with a triumphant flourish.

"I'm exactly where I'm supposed to be," Zane told her quietly. The words and his breath slipped softly along her face and neck, warming her skin as she tilted her head up toward him.

Alyx could feel her heart race. Could feel her breath backing up in her lungs, held prisoner by anticipation.

And then, just as it seemed that Zane was going to back away, he didn't. Instead, he brought his lips down to lightly touch hers.

First contact resulted in a second and then a third, each contact a little more fully realized than the last. Before she realized what she was doing, Alyx threaded her arms around his neck.

In the next heartbeat, she was on her toes, leaning into the man and the kiss as if there were no consequences to consider or to stave off.

Nothing but this moment.

Nothing but him and the seductively delicious taste of his mouth against hers.

Alyx felt light-headed. She leaned even further into Zane, determined to enjoy the ride for however long it would last.

She tasted of something sweet, Zane thought. Sweet

and tempting and kissing her made him want to continue kissing her. Wanting more, not less.

A lot more.

Initially, he'd framed her face, curious as to what a soft, quick pass of her lips would feel like. But rather than satisfy his curiosity, the simple contact had managed to arouse his curiosity to an even higher plane, requiring more.

His hands slipped from her face and enveloped her, bringing her closer to him than a breath. Allowing him to drink her in and get lost in the experience.

And then the door to her apartment suddenly opened.

A bemused blonde stood in the doorway.

"I thought I heard someone out here—" Kady sucked in her breath abruptly as she realized she'd accidentally intruded. "Oh, I'm sorry, I didn't mean to interrupt."

Still holding the door, Alyx's cousin had every intention of withdrawing back into the apartment and closing the door after herself.

Kady started shutting the door, but by then Alyx had pulled back. The latter struggled to bank down the wave of heat that suddenly overtook her. She felt as if her skin was burning up.

"No, wait. You're not interrupting," Alyx protested. It took effort not to stare at the floor, but she forced herself to meet her cousin's eyes dead on. "I was just about to go in," she explained, extremely relieved that she wasn't stuttering. What should have been a very simple act—a kiss, for heaven's sake—had shaken her to the core.

She'd had no idea that Calloway's mouth was so lethal. Her knees were in danger of melting away. How much longer could she have gone on kissing him before she bonelessly sank to the floor and embarrassed herself?

Kady smiled knowingly at Alyx before turning her attention to the man who had been on the other side of her cousin's mouth.

"Hi, I'm Kady. I'm Alyx's cousin and I used to live here."

Zane's somewhat numbed brain scrambled to pull pieces together into some kind of a coherent whole. "You're one of Alyx's doctor cousins," he realized out loud, making the connection.

Extending her hand, Kady grinned broadly at Alyx's companion. "Right. I'm the middle one," she told him. "Kady Pulaski," she said. "At least that's my name when I'm on duty. The rest of the time, I'm Kady Kennedy." She cocked her head, her eyes never leaving his face. "And you are…?"

"On my way out," Zane assured her.

Still holding his hand in a friendly handshake, Kady asked, "Is that hyphenated?"

He knew what she was after. This woman reminded him of Alyx. "My name's Zane Calloway."

Alyx was quick to add, "*Officer* Zane Calloway. He's the policeman who came in response to my 911 call the other night."

"And you came by to follow up on the call?" Kady asked, suppressing a knowing smile.

He was not accustomed to explaining himself. Not

even to his superiors. He did his job beyond reproach and he felt that should be enough for the powers that be—and inquisitive cousins. "Something like that," he murmured.

"Well, come inside," Kady coaxed, opening the door wider and stepping back to admit him and Alyx into the apartment. "Byron's out of town—he's my husband," she told Zane, "and the house is lonely so I thought I'd spend the night with my little cousin and see how things were going for her. But I can always just go over to one of my sisters' houses." She picked up her light blue overnight case she'd left beside the door.

"No, please, stay," Alyx insisted. "It's really not what you think." She quickly slanted a glance at Zane before saying, "He was just dropping me off after a cup of coffee."

This time, Kady didn't bother trying to suppress her grin, and it took over her generous mouth. "Is that what they're calling it these days? I didn't realize I was so out of touch with the current terminology." She noted that Alyx was about to launch into another protest, and she turned her appealing eyes toward Zane. "Really, please don't leave on my account."

Granted he'd entertained the idea—fleetingly—of coming in, but that would lead to complications, he thought. It was better this way. Much better. Alyx's mouth was too sweet for his own good. "I was just bringing Alyx to her door. The doorman isn't around," he tacked on.

There was sympathy in Kady's eyes, and something

more. "Another protective male," she marveled. "What is it about the Pulaski women that brings out the knight in shining armor in men?" she mused aloud. The man she'd eventually married had insisted on being her bodyguard after she'd witnessed his former employer being murdered. "Well, nice meeting you, Officer Zane Calloway," she told him with feeling, then turned toward Alyx. "I'll be in my old room." With that, she picked up her overnight case and walked away.

Alyx could feel herself flushing again. She hadn't thought she was the type to do that until just now. Living in New York City was certainly a learning experience.

"I'm sorry," she apologized.

Zane was unclear as to why she felt it necessary to apologize. "For what?"

"Well, Kady thought that we—" Verbally fumbling, Alyx tried again. "That we were—you know—together," she finally concluded awkwardly for lack of a more descriptive word.

Zane smiled at her in response, and she could almost feel the curve of his mouth work its way deep into her body.

"Maybe for a minute, we were," he told her. Then, to her surprise, Zane lifted the tip of her chin with his thumb, brushed his lips against hers again and murmured "Good night" a beat before he turned away and walked down the hall toward the elevator.

Her heart slammed against her rib cage twice over. The fleeting contact had stirred her insides up almost as much as the full-on, pulling-out-all-the-stops kiss had.

She blew out a breath, feeling drained and exhilarated all at the same time.

Alyx remained standing a moment longer, savoring. Then, pulling herself together, she slipped inside the apartment and closed the door behind her. She threw the lock on for good measure—whether to keep him out or herself in, she wasn't quite sure.

"Kady?" she called, looking around the living room. When she received no answer, she moved into the hall and made her way to the bedrooms. She knocked on the one at the end. "Kady? Are you in there?"

The next moment, her cousin opened the door. Curiosity was evident in the young woman's face, and it was mirrored by the look in her eyes.

"Where's the hunk?" she asked, glancing around.

Alyx offered a slight shrug in response. "On his way home, I imagine."

The expression on Kady's face said that the answer just didn't compute. "Why?"

"Because his shift is over and he lives there?" It came out in the form of a question because Alyx wasn't sure exactly what her cousin was trying to get at.

Kady didn't appear satisfied. Just guilty.

"He really didn't have to leave on my account," Kady told her, leaving her room. "I could have made myself scarce or disappeared altogether. It's not like this kind of thing didn't happen when Sasha, Natalya and I were all living here. It took a bit of juggling, but we managed to work things out."

"He didn't leave on your account," Alyx assured her.

"He really did just come up to walk me to my—to our," she corrected because in her opinion the apartment was more her cousins' than hers, "door. He wasn't planning on coming in. Really."

Kady looked at her much the way a parent looked at a child who had one exceptional trick to their repertoire. "Is that what you honestly think?"

"Yes, I do."

With another melodious laugh, Kady slipped an arm around Alyx's slim shoulders. "Oh, Grasshopper," she teased, "you have much to learn. But I'm here now, so let the teaching begin."

Though having Kady's arm around her comforted her, Alyx drew back slightly. She had to leave no room for doubt about herself and the handsome young patrolman.

"Officer Calloway was the cop who answered my 911 call—"

Kady nodded. "So you said."

"And this morning, he turned up in the ER with a bullet wound. He and his partner had saved a convenience store clerk's life," she added, although it was Zane who'd probably done most of the heavy lifting. There wasn't a scratch on his partner and every hair had been in place. With Zane, only one hair had remained *in* place.

"Heroic, the best kind," Kady declared with approval. Byron had struck her that way from the moment he'd taken charge of the situation. "And he got shot in your vicinity so he could be brought to Patience Memorial, how very thoughtful of him."

"It's not like that," Alyx insisted loyally.

Kady shook her head. "It can *always* be like that," Kady countered. "Life is full of opportunities begging to be taken advantage of. Nowhere does it say that if you're shot, you have to pay your attending ER physician back by practicing CPR on her or by walking them home."

"We drove," Alyx corrected.

"Even better." Kady smiled knowingly. "Trust me, Alyx, he's into you. Now the real question is—" she studied her cousin's face with interest "—are you into him?"

Alyx felt herself shoring up her beaches. "I don't know him."

Now there was a line of bull if she'd ever heard any. "Honey, extensive knowledge isn't necessary in this case—unless he turns out to be a serial killer or an ax murderer—or wears black socks to bed and nothing else," she allowed.

Confusion creased Alyx's brow. "Excuse me?" she asked.

Kady laughed. "Like I said, you have much to learn, and lucky for you, I seem to have a night to kill. Now, the first question I have for you is, is there any ice cream in the freezer?"

Alyx thought for a moment. "I think I saw a half-full container of Spumoni in there—it was there when I moved in and I just haven't gotten around to clearing it out," she confessed.

Kady nodded, approving of the wording that her cousin had used.

"Half-full, not half-empty. Good, that means that you really are one of us. And there's only one way to get rid of ice cream—and throwing it away isn't it," Kady added.

"One of you?" Alyx repeated, still puzzled.

"Yes. An optimist," Kady clarified. "If you were a pessimist like…like…" She tactfully let her voice trail off.

"My mother?" Alyx supplied.

"Well, yes, like your mother," Kady allowed. "Then you wouldn't be a true Pulaski. We see a lemon seed, we're already planning how many glasses of lemonade we can make once it germinates," Kady confided to her. "So, let's bring out the Spumoni, two spoons—your choice on the size—and we'll have a heart-to-heart discussion."

Alyx looked at her warily. She wasn't given to talking about her feelings. Her mother had always discouraged it.

"About?"

"Life, medicine and men," Kady said with a flourish of her hand. "Not necessarily in that order," she added with a conspiratorial wink. "In between, you can tell me how it's going for you in the ER. Is that doctor—" she paused for a moment as she tried to remember the doctor's name "—Gloria something or other still the prime candidate to replace the Wicked Witch of the West, or has she softened up a little in her old age?"

"Gloria Furst," Alyx supplied, then laughed shortly, remembering her last experience with the woman this morning. "I don't think the woman knows how to soften up. She's still hell on wheels and the prime candidate to take the witch's place. Unless she decides to retire sometime soon."

"The undead never retire," Kady told her. "They continue forever and they thrive on the blood of innocent, struggling interns." And then she grinned. "Ah, Grasshopper, let me give you a few tips you might find useful for surviving the curse of the undead…" Kady offered, guiding Alyx toward the kitchen, the Spumoni and salvation.

They were almost out of the living room when they heard the sound of an object crashing against their neighbor's wall. Alyx instantly froze.

Listening.

Waiting for more.

She'd found an excuse to give that waste of skin a piece of her mind and once more to call in the police. This time she would insist that Harry be arrested, even if she had to fabricate testimony. She had the uneasy feeling that Abby, despite a pep talk she'd given the woman in the elevator yesterday morning, would never stand up for herself.

"What's the matter?" Kady asked.

"Our neighbor." She nodded her head toward the other apartment. "He beats his wife."

Kady stiffened, her smile instantly fading. "Are you sure?"

"I've seen the bruises." She was still listening, still waiting. But the crash had no accompanying noise, no raised voices. Nothing but silence came from next door. "I guess maybe he's reined himself in."

"Let's hope so," Kady agreed. "Now, about that ice cream…"

"Already there," Alyx assured her, decreasing the distance between herself and the refrigerator quickly.

"So tell me some more about Officer Hunk," Kady encouraged as she dished out their servings.

Chapter 7

It had been a hectic shift, but a good one, Alyx thought with a smile as she signed out her last patient of the day.

Any shift without Dr. Gloria Furst breathing down her neck, finding fault with everything she did, everything she attempted to do, she considered a good shift. All told, she'd seen forty-one patients today.

And none of them had died.

That, to her, was her ultimate goal: keeping everyone alive and putting them on the path to health, if at all possible. Most of the people she'd dealt with today had been sent home with instructions and, in some cases, with prescriptions.

Three of the forty-one patients had been admitted.

There was the weekend warrior who'd fallen off his ladder as he was painting his house. The man had cracked his thigh, a feat she was still trying to reconcile in her mind. An arm, a leg, this she could understand. But getting one leg caught in the ladder and bringing it and himself down onto the concrete in such a way that he cracked his thigh still mystified her.

There was the octogenarian with what the elderly woman referred to as "heart flutters." She had to be admitted because she was actually in the middle of an unresolved, very mild heart attack and not just a "fluttery episode."

Admitted too had been the four-year-old boy with the one hundred and three fever. But everyone else had been discharged and sent on their way home again, freeing up the beds both in the ER and in the hospital proper.

Despite the hectic pace, Alyx felt pretty satisfied as she started to clock out. God was in his heaven and all was right with the world.

Card in hand, she was about to push it into the slot to register the time of her departure when the ER rear doors—the entrance that all the ambulance attendants used—dramatically burst open. For the most part, the paramedics always staged dramatic entrances, no matter who they brought in or what the patient's actual condition was. It broke up the day.

This time, they actually ran with the gurney, as did the haunted-looking young woman hurrying beside it.

Sobbing, she clutched the hand of the person on the gurney.

As their paths crossed, the young woman looked up at Alyx, tears streaming down her face. "I should have gone over sooner. I should have gone. I *knew* something was wrong. I could feel it in my stomach. Maybe, if I'd gone over earlier, I could have stopped him." She was almost choking on her sobs by now.

Alyx stopped and put her card down.

"Katie," she called over to a nurse who was just approaching the nurse's station from the opposite end of the room. "Could you help out here, please?"

Because no other doctor was in the vicinity, Alyx remained, judging that she could at least assess the case until one of the other physicians on duty became available.

That was when she looked down at the patient on the gurney.

Her pulse instantly quickened as recognition set in. Because of the discoloration, the swelling and the blood, it took her a moment to make the connection. She recognized the clothing before she recognized the beaten face.

"Oh my God," Alyx whispered in stunned disbelief, her eyes widening. She could feel her heart twist in her chest. "Abby," she cried, leaning in over the gurney. "Abby, can you hear me?"

There was a barely discernible flutter of the woman's eyelashes, as if that was the only part of her that could still respond.

Alyx shifted her attention to the young woman who

had come in with her badly beaten neighbor. "What's your name?"

"Beth."

"Where did you find her, Beth?"

The young woman hiccupped as she swallowed her sobs.

"In her apartment. She didn't show up for work this morning and she wasn't answering her phone. I knew that Abby wouldn't just take off like that, so I came over during my break. I rang her bell, but there was no answer so I told the superintendent that I was her sister and I begged him to open up the apartment." She pressed her lips together to try to collect herself. "He did and that was when we found her. On the kitchen floor. She wasn't even bleeding anymore. The blood on her head and face was all crusted and dried."

Beth's smoky-brown eyes were wild as she looked to the ER doctor for answers. "How could he have done that to her? Harry's supposed to love her. She kept telling me that he swore he loved her. You don't do this to someone you love," she insisted.

Alyx frowned and shook her head. "That kind never loves anyone but themselves," she declared angrily. They'd reached the edge of the accessible portion of the ER. "Put her in Trauma Room Three," she told the paramedics, pointing out the location of the room in question.

They eased the gurney into the room, then lined it up with the bed. Alyx got into position with them. "Okay, on my count. One, two, *three,*" she cried. The paramedics, Alyx and one of the attending nurses eased the woman from the gurney onto the hospital bed.

Alyx heard Abby whimper softly.

Like a dog whose spirit had been broken, she thought, shaking her head.

She leaned over the woman as the nurses hooked up monitors. "I'm sorry. Abby, I know it hurts. But I promise you, it's never going to hurt again. *He's* never going to hurt you again," she declared fiercely. Alyx turned to the orderly closest to her. "Get me a camera, Roddy," she instructed. "I need to document all these bruises."

Abby opened the only eye she could. Her left one was temporarily swollen shut.

"No." The single word was hoarsely enunciated through swollen lips. The protest might have been vehement in spirit, but it came out barely audible.

Frustrated, Abby tried to take hold of Alyx's wrist to stop her. "No," she whispered again. "He loves me. He said he was sorry." With each word her voice faded a little more.

Alyx could only feel pity when she looked down at the woman. What she saw this time was worse, far worse than the other two times she'd seen the effects of her neighbor's temper.

"He's not going to hurt you anymore, I promise," she repeated.

But even as she spoke to her, the light went out of Abby's eyes. The nurses had just finished hooking the young woman up to monitors whose sole function was to measure her vital signs.

She was flat-lining.

"Crash cart, I need a crash cart!" Alyx cried. "Stat!"

Beth covered her mouth with her hands to hold back a nervous scream. "What's happening?" she cried, looking at Alyx. There was fear in every syllable. "Is she going to be all right?"

Ordinarily, this was the time that Alyx sugar-coated her answers. She believed in giving a person hope until the last moment. But this time, this time the words that came out of her mouth were unvarnished. And they didn't deal with hope, they dealt with reality, a word she had come to hate at times.

"I don't know," she answered honestly. "But I certainly hope so."

Another one of the nurses came hurrying over with the crash cart and Alyx instantly seized the paddles. Holding them upside down, she waited until Roddy had applied the lubricant to both surfaces and then she yelled out the warning, "Clear," before she applied the paddles to Abby's small chest.

Abby's body convulsed like a marionette whose strings had suddenly all been pulled in one direction, then released. For a split second, part of her body had lost contact with the mattress. And then she fell back down as if the strings had all been cut.

Four more attempts with the paddles yielded the same macabre dance with the same results. The flat line on the monitor remained.

"Dr. Pulaski?" Katie left the rest of her question unspoken but they both knew she was asking her to call the time of death.

Alyx felt her heart twist again inside her chest as if someone was squeezing it.

"No, not yet," she cried. "I can get her back. I can." She resorted to regular CPR, using her fist to pound on Abby's shallow chest rather than simply doing compressions. "C'mon, c'mon. Damn it, Abby, don't let him win," she entreated, frantically trying to raise a response from the woman's heart.

For a moment, there was a glimmer on the monitor and she held her breath, praying that it would continue and grow strong.

But instead, it faded. Alyx felt as if her own heart had stopped as the blip on the monitor returned to a single line. The line eerily continued, emitting a single note that went on indefinitely, sounding an unsettling death knell.

She'd lost her. Abby was gone.

Stepping back, blinking away the tears that filled her eyes, Alyx stripped off her rubber gloves and tossed them in the wastepaper basket. She felt as if she'd just intercepted a direct blow to the gut and found herself struggling not to throw up.

"You did all you could, doctor," the other nurse, Evangeline, an older, grandmotherly woman told her kindly.

"No, I didn't," Alyx retorted between gritted teeth.

She was losing the battle against her emotions. Right now, they were overwhelming her.

"What more could you have done?" Vangie asked.

"I could have insisted the bastard be arrested." Anger bubbled up within her at her passiveness. Alyx thought of the crash she'd heard last night. Had that been Abby? Had Harry, in his rage, flung his wife against the wall? Had Abby been lying on the floor all that time, dying by inches until her friend had discovered her? "I could have gone over last night and demanded to see her when I heard that crash," Alyx cried in frustration. Why hadn't she? she silently demanded. Why?

"What crash?" Abby's friend asked in between heart-wrenching sobs.

But Alyx didn't hear her. She was on her way out of the trauma room, intent on finding the nearest phone. She needed to call the police.

She needed to talk to Zane.

When the call came through over the dispatch line, Ryan answered it because Zane was driving. "Officer Lukkas, what can I do for you, lovely lady?" he asked, flirting with the woman on the other end.

For once, Patrice, the brunette on the other end of the line, was all business. "Tell Officer Calloway he has a call."

Zane could hear Patrice loud and clear. He exchanged glances with Ryan. Private calls over the dispatch line were frowned upon so they were usually turned away. It didn't sound as if that was the case this time.

"A call? You're kidding," Ryan said. "I thought the brass vetoed all personal calls."

"Woman says it's urgent," Patrice told him, then recited, "that she has to get in touch with Calloway. She called it a matter of life or death."

Ryan handed the receiver to Zane. "You get someone pregnant, Calloway?" he asked, raising an eyebrow.

"Not unless I'm doing it in my sleep," Zane replied cryptically.

"More fun when you're awake," Ryan told him, not bothering to suppress a grin.

"So they tell me." One hand on the steering wheel, Zane pressed the button that allowed his voice to be conveyed back to the precinct. "Calloway here."

In the background, he heard dispatch tell someone, "Go ahead, ma'am."

The next moment he heard someone angrily announce, "He killed her."

It took Zane a second to place the voice. Even when he did, he wasn't really sure it was her. He wouldn't have thought that Alyx would have taken the trouble to call him.

"Alyx?" Beside him, Ryan had sat up, noting the change in his partner's tone.

"He killed her," she repeated. There was both anger and agony in her voice. "Did you hear what I just said?" she demanded.

He had questions of his own for her. "Who, Alyx? Who was killed and who did the killing?" Zane asked. He had no idea what she was talking about.

She took a deep breath, trying desperately to remain coherent. "My neighbor. McBride. He killed his wife. They brought her in by ambulance less than an hour ago. I hardly recognized her, he'd beaten her that badly. There was nothing we could do." No, this fell on her. This was *her* loss, *her* fault. "Nothing *I* could do to save her. He killed her," she repeated.

"You sure it was him?"

She took in a breath and released it, then another in an attempt to calm down and remain civil. She pressed on. "They found her in the apartment, on the floor. She'd apparently been there a long time. Beaten to a pulp. So what do you think?"

"Who found her?" Zane asked grimly.

"A friend from work got worried," she recited, then her voice—and her patience—broke. "What does it matter who brought her in? What matters is that he did it." She pressed her lips together to keep from crying. "I should have gone over there last night."

"Why?" he asked, instantly alert. "Did something happen last night after I left?"

She supposed that there was a chance that this wasn't connected to Abby's murder—but she had her doubts. "I heard a crash, something being thrown against the wall. And then there was nothing." She paused for a moment to bank down the sob scratching its way up her throat. "That crash I heard was probably her."

He made no comment on that. He needed to get to her. "Where are you now?"

"At the hospital. But I'm on my way out. I'm going home," she informed him.

Zane filled in the parts she left unspoken. He was beginning to get a handle on the woman. Alyx wasn't going home, she was going to confront her neighbor.

"Don't do anything stupid," he ordered. "Stay at the hospital. I'll take care of this." But the line on the other end had gone dead. "Alyx? Alyx, do you hear me?" he shouted into the receiver.

"Damn it!" Zane bit off a curse as he flung the receiver away from him. The cord all but yanked itself out of the unit. The receiver bounced once, then lay dormant on the floor beside Ryan's feet.

Doing a U-turn, Zane came a hair's breadth away from getting into a nose-to-nose collision with an oncoming car. They both swerved and managed to get out of each other's way enough at the last possible second to remain intact.

"What the hell's going on?" Ryan asked. He grabbed the side strap just above his head to keep from falling into Zane. He was making those turns again, the ones best suited to amusement park rides and that wreaked havoc on stomachs older than twelve. "Where are you going?"

Zane rattled off Alyx's address to his partner. He could all but see Ryan processing it. "Remember the doctor who sewed me up in the ER?"

"Remember her?" Ryan repeated with an incredulous laugh. "That doc's just in every dream I've had since then."

Speeding up, he blasted the siren even louder, anxious to be there. "She just called to tell me that she's just pronounced her neighbor dead, the one whose husband she'd said kept using her as a punching bag. Abby something-or-other." He needed to get that information before he met with Alyx again. He had a hunch his not remembering the woman's last name would definitely rub Alyx the wrong way.

"Shouldn't we be heading to the hospital to take statements?" Ryan suggested.

"She's on her way to the building to confront the bastard," he repeated, waiting for Ryan to catch on to what he was saying.

Slowly it dawned on his partner. "And you're afraid that this guy is going to wind up hurting her, too," Ryan concluded.

"No," he bit off bluntly. "I'm afraid she's going to shoot him," Zane answered flatly. "And if she does, or gets hurt, it'll be my fault."

Ryan felt lost again. He looked at his partner through squinting eyes, trying to focus not just his vision, but also his mind. "Just how do you figure that?"

Zane was losing his patience. But it was himself he was irritated with, not Ryan. "Because I didn't take the report seriously. I thought the wife was just saying that he abused her to get her husband in trouble. You know, her word against his, that kind of thing. But in these cases, the courts usually take the woman's side."

"So you've decided that you're going to be championing the underdog?" Ryan guessed.

Before answering, Zane thought of his father. He recalled how broken and dispirited the man had been the last time he'd seen him. A week later, his father committed suicide.

"Yeah," he said, sealing in his emotions, "something like that."

"Very noble of you," Ryan commented, then added under his breath, "If you don't wind up killing us first." Ryan held on to the strap with both hands.

Chapter 8

"I don't think I can walk a straight line," Ryan complained as he slid out of the passenger side of the squad car and rose shakily to his feet.

For a moment, he braced his hand against the roof, trying to get his bearings and waiting for his knees to snap in. The twists and turns Zane had taken to get here had made him feel as if he was inside of a blender set on "high."

"Who the hell taught you how to drive? Some NASCAR wannabe?" he demanded, facing Zane. "A couple of turns back there, I'm not sure if all four wheels were even on the ground."

"I'll let you drive next time," Zane tossed over his shoulder.

He didn't bother to turn around to look at Ryan. Instead, he hurried over to the hospital's ER entrance. He'd had a change in plans after calling the hospital and asking if Alyx had left yet. She hadn't. Because he needed information about Abby's condition upon arrival, getting to the hospital first made more sense. So he'd gotten to Patience Memorial in record time to head Alyx off before she had a chance to go home.

They'd had to park one lot over and now Ryan was practically running to keep up. "You bet I'll drive. We might get there five seconds later, but we'll get there in one piece."

A couple of steps short of the entrance, Zane stopped and turned around. Holding out his arms he made a show of looking himself over. "Don't see any loose pieces here."

"*This* time," Ryan said grudgingly through gritted teeth.

"Sorry, I've got too much going on to spend time worrying about what *might* happen the next time. That can be your job," he told his partner.

Walking into the ER, he strode past both the sign-in desk and the registration area. Ryan followed in his wake, flashing an apologetic smile at the woman sitting behind the registration desk.

When it became clear that they weren't stopping, she rose to her feet and called after them. "Officers! Officers, can I help you?"

Zane was fairly confident that he could help himself and kept going. He went through the electronic doors that led to where the patients were treated. Scanning the vicinity, he came up empty. There were a lot of curtained beds and a smattering of rooms. Alyx could be in any one of them. He didn't have time for this.

Zane grabbed the first person in scrubs who crossed his path, a young, heavyset orderly who looked as if he would have no trouble picking up a fallen patient and carrying him or her back to their bed—with one hand.

"Excuse me," Zane said in response to the silent question on the younger man's face. "I'm looking for Dr. Pulaski."

The orderly continued looking at him quizzically. "Which one?"

"How many of them are there?" Ryan asked, coming up behind Zane.

The orderly paused to do a mental count. "At last count, we had six. They tell me more are on the way. They've got enough to open up their own hospital," the orderly said with a laugh.

Six doctors in one family—it didn't seem possible. He wondered who got to carve the turkey at Thanksgiving. "She works in the ER. Blond hair, blue eyes, stands about this tall." He held his hand up to his shoulder. "Her name's Alyx—"

The orderly's face lit up with recognition. "Oh, her. Yeah, she was here." He looked quickly around the immediate area. "But I thought she went off duty."

Zane shook his head. "She just called me from the ER. It was about a patient of hers who died today."

The added information didn't seem to ring a bell for the orderly. He apparently hadn't been part of the team working with Alyx.

"Okay, then maybe she's still around here somewhere." The orderly pointed toward a desk that looked like an island in a sea of beds. "They can tell you more at the nurses' station."

"Thanks." With a quick nod, Zane started toward the desk.

"Zane!"

He stopped dead when he heard her call his name. He would have recognized her voice anywhere, even in its present state. Pain and anger throbbed within every letter.

Zane barely had time to turn toward her voice before she was all but in his face.

"Come with me." Alyx struggled to keep the tremor out of her voice. Abby's death had affected her more than she'd thought it would. "Abby is still in the trauma room."

Leading the way, when she approached the doorway of the trauma room, Alyx hung back and allowed Zane and Ryan to enter the room first.

"Oh my God," Ryan whispered, appearing utterly sobered by the sight of just how badly the young woman lying on the hospital bed had been beaten.

Alyx's attention was focused entirely on Zane. She waited to see his reaction. Would he just shrug Abby's death off, hardened by what he had to deal with on the streets, or would the plight of this poor young woman—hardly more than a girl—get to him?

Zane gave no indication of what was going on in his head as he approached the body, saying nothing. She kept her eyes on his profile, which was how she saw the slight twitch of a muscle in his cheek.

Abby's death wasn't just "business as usual" for the man, she thought, relieved that he apparently felt something, no matter how hard he tried to appear stoic.

It made her feel a little closer to him, which was a good thing because right now, she needed to feel close to someone. She felt far too vulnerable to be by herself and she couldn't quite see herself running to her aunt and uncle.

"He killed her, Zane," she said quietly, repeating what she'd told him earlier. "As surely as if he'd aimed a gun at her head. Except that it was more personal than a gun. He beat the life out of her with his fists—and he could literally *feel* it happening, could *feel* the life draining out of her." Gritting her teeth, she ground out her declaration. "The man is an absolute monster."

He saw no point in disagreeing with Alyx. Turning away, he instructed, "Don't let anyone touch her. The medical examiner's going to want to perform a thorough autopsy."

"More indignities," she murmured, looking down at Abby. A person's body shouldn't have to be cut up like pieces of a jigsaw puzzle after they'd died. There should be some kind of nobility maintained in death.

But not for victims, she thought sadly.

"I don't think she's in a position to mind," Zane told her, his voice unusually kind. "Besides, we need more evidence than just proximity and say-so to nail the bastard who did this to her." He'd been around the people in the information-gathering unit enough times to know how they worked. "The CSI unit is going to want to go over her—and the room where she was found."

Alyx struggled to hold on to the numbness at the center of her core. Once that was gone, this morning's events would hit her. Hard. "Her friend said it was the kitchen."

Zane began to walk out of the room. Ryan paused for a moment longer to look at the shell that was left on the bed. He shook his head. Suddenly aware that he'd fallen behind and that Zane wasn't the type to wait, Ryan hurried to catch up.

Alyx was already out of the room and shadowing Zane's steps.

"Are you going to arrest him?" she asked, breaking the silence.

He selected a place, an alcove, that was out of the way of the general foot traffic. He nodded toward Ryan, who took his cue and pulled out his phone to call CSI. Only then did he address Alyx's question. "I'm going to bring him in for questioning."

"And then you'll arrest him," she concluded, unwilling to accept anything less than that.

He'd learned not to make promises that weren't up to him to keep. "That depends on what the detectives find.

Innocent until proven guilty, remember?" He saw the way she fisted her hands at her sides. It wasn't hard to interpret her body language. "It's frustrating," he agreed, "but that's the way the system works. Most of the time it's a pretty decent system."

"Right." She nodded, trying to find solace in the thought that Abby's husband was going to be brought to justice, although she would have preferred to get ten minutes alone with him where she could do to his face what he had done to Abby's.

Behind her, she heard Zane's partner on the phone with their precinct, notifying the homicide division about the body in Patience Memorial's Trauma Room Three.

She couldn't stop the shiver that snaked its way down her spine.

Taking her by the arm, Zane moved her aside, away from Ryan and everyone else. "Are you going to be all right?" he asked.

She took a breath to steady her nerves, hating that she had to resort to that. She should be stronger.

"I will be," she said out loud. "The minute you throw that rotten scum into a holding cell." Tears suddenly formed again and she blinked several times to drive them away. "I feel like I failed her."

If anyone had dropped the ball here, he thought, it had been him. Because of his preconceived notions about women accusing their husbands of abusing them. A good cop went with gut feelings, not agendas. The lesson he'd learned today shouldn't have been at this young woman's expense.

"You can't take care of everyone, Alyx. First and foremost, *she* failed herself." He did believe that. Believed that everyone had it in them to be master of their own destiny. "Nobody told her she had to stay and be that guy's punching bag."

Alyx had gotten to talk to Beth, Abby's friend, while waiting for Zane to arrive. She'd managed to get a little information about Abby.

"She had no one to turn to, Zane. The one time she tried to leave him—the woman who found her in her apartment let Abby stay with her—he threatened to kill them both. Her friend got scared. And so did Abby."

That still wasn't an excuse. "A shelter for abused women would have taken her in."

That had such a depressing sound, she thought. "Maybe Abby wasn't aware of that. Or maybe she was too ashamed to go to one. She was probably afraid that the bastard would find her and make a scene there as well. He's a big man," she recalled. "At least physically," she added with no small contempt.

Zane nodded. Looking over her head, he saw that Ryan had ended his call.

"We'll find the evidence to put him away," Zane promised her. "I've got to get going." He wasn't needed here any longer. "I've got to get this bastard before he takes off."

Now he was talking. She nodded and fell into place

beside him, forcing Ryan to trail behind slightly. "I'm coming with you."

He almost stopped dead, but he couldn't afford to lose more time. "I don't want you—"

"I'm off duty and I live in the apartment next door. You can't stop me from going home, Officer Calloway."

"Home" was not her destination and they both knew it. "All right, but I want you to stay out of the way. This could get ugly."

"It already *is* ugly," she countered heatedly. "But don't worry, I don't intend to interfere with police procedure. I'll be there to applaud it," she told him.

He had his doubts about that, but she was right. He couldn't stop her from going home.

Because he wanted to keep an eye on her, Zane took her to her building in the squad car. Ryan drove while he rode shotgun and Alyx sat in the back. She was eerily quiet. Ryan did most of the talking.

Zane couldn't remember a single thing that was said.

The door to the apartment next door to hers was unlocked and ajar. After pushing open the door, Zane took a long, sweeping appraisal of the apartment. It resembled the aftermath of a raging storm where all contents had been trashed.

He slanted a look at Alyx. "And you only heard that one crash?" It didn't seem possible to achieve this level of destruction so quickly.

She was as confused as he was. "Just that. Nothing else. My cousin spent the night. She didn't mention hearing anything else either. You can ask Marja yourself."

They would get to that in time. "I believe you," he said. Leaving Ryan to process what he saw, Zane walked into the couple's bedroom.

More chaos there.

The closet door was open all the way. Only Abby's clothes remained. "Looks like this Harry character might have taken off." He turned to look at Alyx. "Do you know where he works?"

"I don't even know *if* he works," she answered. She knew very little about the man other than he gave her the creeps and that he beat his wife.

They heard voices coming from the other room. Instantly alert, Zane waved her behind him as he drew out his service revolver. But she'd be damned if she would hang back the way he silently indicated. If that monster was back, she wanted to accuse him to his face, not cower in the shadows.

It took restraint not to sprint ahead of Zane but to walk behind him.

Walking into the living room, braced to confront Abby's killer, Alyx was completely surprised to see a familiar face instead.

"Tony," she cried in surprise. Turning away from his partner, her oldest cousin's husband appeared relieved to see her.

When she threw her arms around his neck, he returned

her embrace. There was a time when he wouldn't have. When he would have stepped away from the greeting because it made him uncomfortable. But Sasha was slowly indoctrinating him in the ways of passionate Poles and—God help him—he was even beginning to like it.

"I went numb when I saw the address," he confessed. "I was trying to figure out how to tell the family that something had happened to you. Dispatch got the apartment number wrong," he explained.

"Hard to get good help these days," Ryan commented as he joined the group.

Alyx offered the homicide detective a grateful smile. "No, I'm okay."

Detective Anthony Santini looked down at this newest member of the family. A slight frown creased his lips. "You don't look okay," he observed.

Maybe more of her feelings were showing than she thought. "The woman died on my watch."

"Did you know her?" he asked.

Alyx shook her head. "Not very well." She glanced toward Zane. "Just enough to know that she was being abused."

"But not enough to talk her into leaving," Tony guessed. His tone was nonjudgmental.

It didn't matter. She still felt guilty that she hadn't taken more of an active stand to help the woman. "I saw her in the elevator the other day, a fresh bruise on her arm. I told her she didn't have to take it, that she had every right to stand up for herself." Obviously, that hadn't been enough. "Maybe I should have made her stay with me. She might still be alive if I had."

"There's a reason they call it hindsight," Tony told her. "Don't beat yourself up," he advised. "It's not going to change anything anyway." Tony looked over her head at the patrolman who seemed to be with her. "Officer—?"

"Calloway," Zane supplied. "And that's Officer Lukkas. We've already called in the CSI unit to the hospital."

Tony nodded. "We're going to need a second detail here. But, for a matter closer to home—Officer Calloway, could you see to it that my wife's cousin isn't alone right now?"

Zane nodded as if he had just been given another routine assignment. "No problem, Detective."

"And see that she eats," Tony requested as an afterthought. "The Pulaski women have a tendency not to eat when they're stressed or upset. It drives their mother crazy," he added, thinking of his mother-in-law. "It makes it doubly hard for Magda since she now runs a restaurant and either oversees or takes care of over eighty percent of the cooking for all the households."

With that, Tony turned on his heel and began to set about the business of making a case against Abby's husband.

"You heard the detective," Zane said to Alyx, ushering her out of the neighbor's apartment and to her own door. "We need to get you something to eat."

The last thing on her mind was food. "He just wants me out of the way," she protested.

"That, too." Zane didn't bother disputing it. "But he still had a point about eating." The woman, he noted, had a knock-out figure, but it wouldn't take much to get her to the skinny level. And that, he thought, would be a crying shame.

She was too old to be force-fed, Alyx thought. "I'm not hungry."

He wasn't about to accept any excuses. "Doesn't matter."

"Besides, I need to get my car," she reminded him. "You made me leave the family car in the hospital parking structure." The repairs on it, mercifully, had been minor and she'd picked the vehicle up at lunch time.

He merely nodded. "There was a reason for that."

"Care to share?" she prodded, willing to sacrifice a little to gain what she was waiting for.

But he wasn't about to elaborate, at least not yet. "Don't change the subject." His eyes narrowed as he looked at her. "All right, if you won't let the food come to you, then I'll take you to the food." He paused to tell Ryan that he was leaving for the next forty-five minutes to an hour to get her car, but that he would be back.

Ryan put his own interpretation to what his partner had just said.

"You're just trying to get out of canvassing the area," Ryan complained. Canvassing required dedication, good shoe wear and a particularly hard skin because of all the insults and verbal abuse people would fling at him. He braced himself for the ordeal that lay ahead.

"Hey, the detective gave me this assignment," Zane said in defense of his actions. In response, Ryan just waved him on as he went to knock on his first door.

"Maybe you should stay and help him," Alyx said. "I can get a cab back to the hospital—or walk. It isn't all that far."

"Lukkas likes to complain. If I help him, that means he won't have anything to carry on about. It's better this way, trust me. Besides, you look like you could use the company."

She chewed on her lower lip for a moment before responding. "I've never had anyone die in front of me like that before."

"But you're a doctor," he protested.

She shook her head. "Doesn't matter. I still never had anyone die in front of me." She let out a shaky breath. "It's pretty awful."

He could sympathize. One didn't get used to death so easily, and maybe that was a good thing, otherwise, a certain jadedness took over.

"There's no real way to prepare for it," he told her. "But once it happens, you just have to make yourself move on."

"Doesn't seem right, me moving on. Abby can't."

"Think of her being in a better place," he advised. When she looked up at him, he could see the surprise in her eyes. "What?" he asked.

"Nothing. I just didn't take you for the type to say something like that," she told him honestly.

He wasn't aware that he was a "type." He'd spent so many years walking to his own drummer, he thought that would have broken him out of any kind of mold.

"Why?" Humor curved Zane's mouth. "Because I carry around a pitchfork?" he deadpanned.

"No, I just didn't think you believed in anything you couldn't see with your own eyes," she said quietly.

"I guess that makes me a complex person."

"I guess it does," she agreed.

The elevator arrived and she walked in first. Abby's death was still as horrible as it had been a few moments ago, but she took solace in Zane's presence. Though she couldn't explain why or put it into coherent words, he made her feel…better.

Chapter 9

Alyx glanced at her rearview mirror.

The black and white squad car, with Zane behind the wheel, was still there, following her.

Was he planning to come all the way back to her apartment building? He'd dropped her off at the hospital parking structure, stopping right beside her vehicle, a hand-me-down she'd inherited from her cousins who'd all owned and driven the car at one time or another. Once she started up the car, she'd assumed that the policeman would return to the precinct.

But he didn't.

Instead, he followed her out of the structure and turned the squad car toward her building. Alyx didn't know what to make of it until she remembered that his partner was probably still in her building, knocking on neighbors' doors and trying to find out if anyone had seen or heard anything that might help them bring charges against Abby's husband.

Turning at the corner, Alyx pulled into the underground structure next to her building and parked the car in the spot that coincided with her apartment number. She noted that Zane parked the black and white in the loading and unloading zone reserved for deliveries and emergency vehicles.

When she got out of her car, he was already crossing to her.

"I guess you're here to pick up your partner," she speculated, searching for something to say as they got on the elevator together.

Her words sounded stilted to her ear. She definitely wasn't at her best, but that was because she still felt numb and completely disoriented. The ordeal in the Trauma Room had felt almost surreal to her. She'd lost her grasp on her bearings and it would take a bit of work to smooth things out in her head. She kept seeing Abby's pain-filled eyes in her mind.

"Lukkas is probably long gone by now," Zane answered. "I doubt if he found all that many people in at this time of day and his shift ended a while back."

Something didn't add up. "Don't you have the same shift?"

"Yes." The elevator stopped on every floor, taking on passengers or dropping them off. It would have been faster to take the stairs, he thought. But one glance at her face told him that she was far too drained for such exertion.

She connected the dots, albeit in slow motion. "So that means that you're off duty, too."

He stepped closer to her as a woman with a fluffy dog—the only breed he knew for certain was a German shepherd and this wasn't it—pressed to her ample chest came in. "Yes."

He was in her space. And getting more so without moving an inch. She tried to keep her mind on the conversation and not the way her skin was heating.

"I don't understand. If you're not picking up your partner, what are you doing here?"

He thought it was easier to take shelter in the excuse he'd been handed. "Detective Santini told me to keep you company." The woman and her dog got out on the next floor. Both Zane and Alyx breathed a sigh of relief. Zane moved back but not far enough to negate his presence. Alyx could still feel the impression of his body, even though there was now space between them.

"Detective Santini is my cousin's husband and he tends to worry. Worrying is the official family hobby, I'm told," she informed him. "If that's all that's making you stay here, consider yourself unshackled. You're free to go home, Officer Calloway," she informed him.

No, he wasn't. He wasn't any more free to do that than he was to turn a blind eye to transgressions of the law. Not even if he wanted to.

"Maybe that's not all that's making me stay," he told

her as the elevator came to a slow, grinding halt on the fifth floor.

"Oh?"

Why had her mouth suddenly gone so dry? And why was she behaving like some kind of pubescent, inexperienced preteen? She was way past that. Especially after what had gone down today at the ER. Seeing death that close made a person grow up.

Fast.

What was wrong with her? Alyx scolded herself. But even as she did so, she heard herself asking Zane, "Then what else is making you stay?" A straight line. She was feeding him a straight line. In hopes of what? Something to flatter her ego? To reaffirm her worth after having her esteem all but flattened today?

She had no answers. She waited to hear his.

Zane took the keys out of her hand and unlocked her door. As he did so, she glanced over toward Abby's apartment. The CSI unit had apparently cleared out, leaving the infamous yellow tape in their wake, warning everyone in the vicinity not to trespass past the makeshift barriers.

Another salvo of guilt exploded within her.

"You," she heard Zane say.

Blinking, her attention zeroed in on Zane as the temperature in the hallway rose by another ten degrees. It was as if someone had just shoved her into an oven.

"You look like you need company," he explained, twisting the knob on her door and opening it for her. He stepped back and let her enter her apartment first.

He was right, she thought. She didn't want to be alone right now, but her only alternative was to call up one of her cousins and she didn't want to sound like some fresh, dewy-eyed innocent who needed babysitting. She admired them, wanted to be like them. The last thing she wanted was for them to think of her as some weak, clingy creature who needed pampering.

Not to mention that her uncle was just searching for an excuse to have her come live at the house in Queens. Her aunt and uncle were lovely, lovely people and she adored them already. But they both had a tendency to be overly protective. She wasn't used to that. Her mother wasn't like that.

Her mother was the exact opposite, taking marginal interest in her daughters unless it came to something that presented itself as a competition with Josef's family. Then her mother was right there, in the thick of it. Pushing and advising.

"Really, I'll be all right," she told Zane. "You probably have things you want to do."

He closed the door and his eyes met hers. "I do."

Breathe, Alyx, breathe! she ordered herself. "Well, then—"

Zane paused to flip the lock on the door, then turned around to face her. "I'm doing it," he informed her.

"Babysitting the detective's cousin-in-law?" she questioned. *This* was what he wanted to do?

"Is that how you see yourself?" he asked. "'The detective's cousin-in-law'?" he echoed. "Because I don't."

"Okay," she said gamely. "How do you see me?" Did that just come out of her? Was that her playing coy?

Since when?

"I see you as somebody who shouldn't be alone right now because you tend to overthink things." Because he found himself wanting to touch her, to trace the contours of her face with his fingertips to reassure himself that she was here, and real, he took a step back.

"They say it takes one to know one." The words came slowly.

What was he doing to her? Why was it suddenly so hard to function? Where was her spirit, damn it? Where was her anger? Both kept her safe and isolated. But she couldn't seem to summon either.

A glimmer of a smile curved Zane's mouth. "Maybe you're right," he agreed, terminating the discussion.

He crossed to the kitchen and opened the refrigerator and then the freezer. The latter appeared amply stocked, while the former was not.

He glanced at her over his shoulder. "You eat anything else except ice cream?"

She just hadn't had time to go grocery shopping. Maybe on the weekend… "On occasion."

He reviewed what else was in the main section of the refrigerator. There was a carton of eggs with only one egg missing and a container of parmesan cheese. A quick glance into her pantry showed some oil, a package of flavored bread crumbs and a packet of cough drops.

"Well," he concluded, stepping away from the pantry,

"I can make us a large omelet, or we can order out. Your choice."

She stared at him incredulously. "You cook?" she asked.

"Why does that surprise you so much?" he asked. "Men cook."

"The only ones I know have their own cooking shows on cable channels."

There was no point in debating this. He cooked, end of story. He moved on. "You didn't answer my first question. Do you want me to make us a couple of omelets, or do you want—"

When she wasn't at Aunt Magda's, sampling the end results of her exquisite culinary skills, she was buying takeout. This would be a pleasant change—as long as it didn't put Zane out too much. "Omelet sounds good," she said, interrupting him.

"Omelet it is," he said with feeling.

The next moment, he was opening up cabinets and drawers, looking for a frying pan, plates and utensils.

Slipping in next to him, Alyx produced the items one at a time, then set them down on the counter before him and next to the stove.

He took over like a pro. She watched him for a moment, then, curious, asked, "Your mother teach you how to cook?"

He laughed shortly, mainly to himself. "By default. I guess you could say that."

Alyx shook her head. "I'm afraid I don't understand what that means."

"My mother was too busy to cook for us." Among other things, he thought. Had it not been for the money from his father's life insurance policy, they would have all wound up on the street or living out of his mother's old Ford station wagon. "Someone had to do it, so I did," he concluded carelessly.

She got the impression that his mother was some sort of a dedicated professional. Even so, how could a mother neglect her own children like that? "What was she so busy doing?"

"Drinking."

The answer, fired like a bullet, startled her. For a second, she didn't know how to react. She'd obviously stumbled blindly onto a very sensitive topic. He should have given her some kind of warning.

"Oh. I'm sorry," she apologized, feeling awkward as hell. "I didn't mean to pry."

Yeah, she did, Zane thought, but he guessed he owed her one. Owed it because his take on the situation next door had kept him from, at the very least, taking the husband in for a cooling-off period. Maybe if he had, there wouldn't be any yellow tape sealing off the door.

"My mother drank to forget," he said, half to himself, half to her as he took the carton of eggs out of the refrigerator and proceeded to break them, one by one, over a bowl.

The words he'd uttered just seemed to hang in the air, waiting to be clarified.

"Forget what?" Alyx finally asked in a hushed voice,

her insatiable curiosity urging her on. However, that didn't prevent her from feeling as if she treaded on a rickety bridge stretched out over a ravine. Her adrenaline raced madly.

"To forget that she was the reason my father killed himself," he answered as he poured the mixture into the preheated pan. A sizzling noise marked the meeting of eggs and oil.

"Oh my God, I'm so sorry," she repeated, wishing she could say something more meaningful. "I didn't realize—"

He shrugged it away, curtailing her discomfort. "I know." He put down the fork he used to beat the eggs together. "I didn't push the investigation into your second-hand allegations about McBride beating his wife because I thought it was a ruse."

When he paused, Alyx didn't press him with questions or take offense at what he'd said. She just waited for him to tell her the rest of it at his own pace.

After a moment, her patience was rewarded.

"That was the excuse my mother used to get back at my father. He stepped out on her—or so she thought— and she wanted to get back at him the only way she knew how. With his kids. So she made up this whole story, even had a friend hit her a few times so that there were bruises to photograph. She won custody of us easily.

"What she hadn't counted on," he continued grimly, resuming cooking, "was that this was going to break my father. Being separated from his sons was more than he could take. He started drinking when he got home from work to fill the emptiness at night. He expanded the hours he drank until, eventually, he started showing up at work drunk. His superior told him he had to choose between work and the bottle. My father punched him out."

He glanced at her and saw that her eyes had widened with compassion. Without fully understanding why, he felt grateful to her.

Taking the lid off the frying pan, he mixed in what little cheese and then breadcrumbs he had available to him, then returned the lid to the pan while lowering the temperature.

"The next thing he knew, my father wasn't a cop anymore. Being a cop and our dad was all he ever knew how to be," he told her, struggling to hold his feelings in check. This had happened a long time ago. "Without that, my father thought he was nothing. So he sat down, wrote it all down in a letter for my mother to read, and then, just like that, he put the gun barrel into his mouth and blew his brains out."

The only sound in the kitchen was the sizzling of the omelet as it cooked. Alyx hardly breathed.

Zane pushed on. He'd come this far, he might as well get it all out this one time. Maybe it was even good for him to unburden himself this way.

"After she read my father's letter, my mother just fell apart. Guilt I guess. She started drinking, too." He punctuated the revelation with a half shrug. "So it was up to me to take care of my two younger brothers, my mother and myself."

She felt her heart ache for him. "And you were ten?"

Zane thought for a moment, trying to remember. It felt like another lifetime. "Around that age. Maybe eleven."

"No one should have to go through something like that as a kid," she cried.

Watching the omelet, Zane laughed shortly. "There's never a good age to watch your parents self-destruct," he pointed out. "But I got through it."

She noticed that he'd only mentioned himself. "And your brothers?"

Growing up, Billy had always been the delicate one, the one who could never roll with the punches. The one he'd always tried to protect. Eddie just cut himself off from all of them, existing in his own little world. The minute he graduated high school, he was gone. He had no idea where Eddie was now.

"Not so much," he told her honestly. "One brother just disappeared when he turned eighteen, the other seems to be under the impression that alcohol or drugs—or some combination thereof—can erase all his problems. He hits bottom, swears he's learned his lesson and promises to straighten out and fly right."

He moved the frying pan off the burner but still left the lid on it. "And for a while, he does. Until something else blows up on him, or he thinks it blows up on him, and then it starts all over again. The games and the lies—" He stopped abruptly and glared at her. "How did this turn into a therapy session?"

"You wanted to talk about it," Alyx answered him quietly.

Zane looked at her as if she'd lost her mind. Where the hell had she gotten that idea? "No, I didn't."

Her eyes met his. "I haven't known you all that long, Zane, but I've already learned one important thing about you. That if you don't want to do something, you don't do it. Isn't that what you said earlier?" she reminded him. "That if you didn't want to do something or be somewhere, then you didn't or you wouldn't?" She waited for him to deny it.

Zane blew out a breath. She had him. "You listen to everything I say?"

Her mouth curved. "One of my better qualities," Alyx quipped. As she watched, Zane removed the lid from the frying pan and set it aside. "So, is there anything I can do to help?"

"Yeah. You could've learned how to stock your refrigerator with a few more things so I could have made this omelet interesting," he suggested.

"You already have," she said, her mind on what he'd just told her about his childhood. It couldn't have been easy, talking about that. "I could go to the store if you want," she offered. The next moment, she was heading toward the front of the apartment and the door. "There's this deli around the corner—"

He held his hand up, calling her back. "Too late. This is just about done," he told her.

The containers that had held the flavored breadcrumbs and the parmesan cheese were lined up on the counter, empty. He would have put in a drop of milk as well, if she'd had it. There was a small container of creamer, for her coffee he imagined, but it was presweetened with French vanilla flavoring and the taste would have been all wrong for the omelet.

Testing the consistency of the omelet with the side of his spatula, he was satisfied with its firmness. "Dinner's ready," he announced.

Zane flipped the omelet over to its other side. The first side had already reached a golden brown. It took the second side half the time to reach the same color.

Zane deposited the giant omelet onto a plate, cut it in half and then slid one of the halves onto the second plate.

"Dig in," he told her, moving the plate in front of her, "so I can tell Detective Santini that I followed his orders down to the letter and made sure you ate."

"You looking for a promotion?" Alyx teased, sliding onto the stool beside him.

"If it comes, I'll take it," he told her. "After all, that's the goal, isn't it? You work hard so you can advance."

She studied him for a moment. She had a hunger to know things about this man, she realized. And not just so that she could make conversation more easily. "Is that what you want to be, a detective?"

"What I want to be," he told her with honest sincerity, "is happy." Something he'd decided a long time ago that he could never be. It wasn't in the cards. His father hadn't been happy and neither had his mother. As for Billy, well, if he was even halfway up that road, he wouldn't be trying to anesthetize himself all the time. And who knew where Eddie was? Or even if he was. For all he knew, Eddie was dead. Why should he be the lucky one? What made him so special to merit the prize?

"That sounds doable," Alyx replied.

"It's harder than you might think," he countered. "Especially considering the kind of gene pool I have working against me."

"Happiness isn't the result of a gene pool," she told him. "Happiness is something that's inside everyone. You just have to not be afraid to let it out."

He stopped eating and looked at her. Talk about a Pollyanna attitude. "Wow. What color's the sky in your world, lady?"

"Blue. Just like yours." And then she grinned as she looked down at her plate. The omelet was almost gone. She'd almost finished it without realizing. "This is good," she pronounced. "You're a good cook. See, a bad situation turned good in one small way."

"Thanks," he murmured in response to her compliment. At the same time, he disregarded the rest of her statement.

What he wasn't prepared for was the tiny sliver of warmth he experienced in response to her praise. There and gone within a heartbeat, he had to admit that it still felt good.

Very, very good.

Chapter 10

When the time came to leave, Zane found himself reluctant to go for a number of reasons. Only one of which had to do with Alyx's safety.

He'd never been one to believe in the endless stories in praise of "chemistry," predominantly because he had never really experienced the effects himself. Desire, yes, temporary attraction that, stripped down, was really more about basic, sexual arousal, yes, but chemistry? No. He'd never found himself in its crosshairs.

Chemistry implied that something unusual, something almost magical or mystical, was happening, involving all the senses plus a mysterious "X-factor" that managed to fill up all the nooks and crannies of a person's existence. That had never been the case for him.

But he had to admit that if he allowed himself to lower his guard, to open himself up the way he refused to ever since his parents had split, the woman could really get to him. In some fashion, shape or form, she had already gotten to him.

Or at least had begun to.

Which was all the more reason to leave.

And also a reason to stay.

He forced himself to his feet, leaving the counter and his empty plate.

"I'd better get going," he told her. And still he hesitated. "Are you going to be all right?" he asked abruptly.

"You mean am I going to sleep with the light on?" She gave a casual little shrug. "Maybe. Is what happened last night just next door to me while I went about my life going to haunt me? For at least a while, yes, it will. Is either situation something that anyone can help with? No," she told him honestly. "I'm going to have to work all that out for myself."

He looked at her closely, searching her face. "So you're not worried?"

That had come out of left field and she wasn't following him. Alyx cocked her head. "About…?"

Maybe this little talk was a bad idea. He shouldn't have begun to press the issue. If she wasn't afraid, he had no right to open up this can of worms and possibly put the idea of fear into her head.

"That you're not going to be able to sleep." At the last moment he grasped at a straw and threw it at her, hoping she didn't think he was crazy—or question him further. If he thought he'd been successful with the eleventh-hour substitution, he was sadly mistaken.

"That's not what you meant," she told him as if she could see right into his head. "The only reason you would use the word 'worried' is if you were asking me if I was afraid that Harry hadn't skipped the state and was going to come after me because, in his twisted mind, he somehow blames me for his wife's death. Maybe even thinks that I drove him to it somehow."

By the look on Zane's chiseled face, she'd guessed right. Alyx grinned. "You look surprised."

He supposed he was. He wasn't accustomed to civilians being clearheaded. "If you ever decide you don't want to be a doctor, you'd make one hell of an investigative cop."

"So I take it I guessed right?" she asked with a knowing smile.

He nodded. "Look, I could hang around for a while," he offered. "You know, keep watch from the sofa if it would make you feel more secure."

He was serious, she thought. That was rather nice. But unnecessary. "I'm not the one who's worried," she pointed out. "Besides, I just made a simple suggestion to her. I never got Abby to register a complaint against him. If anything, I got her to cling to him even more."

He waved his hand dismissively at her words. "You're talking as if McBride is operating with a logical mind. He isn't. In his mind, he might even hold you responsible for what happened because Abby might have mentioned something to him like, 'Maybe I should file abuse charges against you like Alyx said.' And because he has a volatile temper, that would have been enough to make him lose it and start beating her up. That would be all it would have taken—and your name was invoked, which is what he would remember."

"What's going to make tomorrow different?" Alyx asked.

Zane watched at her, confused as to what that had to do with anything.

"Maybe he's going to lie low now, but he'll work himself up and wind up coming tomorrow night," she explained. "Or maybe he'll restrain himself for a while and come to even the score with me next week. Are you going to plant yourself in my living room and take root here for the unforeseeable future?" she asked. "He might even turn out to be the patient type and won't strike for a couple of months."

"Are you deliberately trying to scare yourself—and me?" he added. What she'd just described would be like living with a time bomb that could go off at any time—or not.

"No," she explained, "I'm trying not to entertain any fear right from the start. If I give in tonight, then it'll be that much harder to face being alone tomorrow night, and the night after that—"

"So maybe you should move in with one of those doctor cousins of yours," he told her. "There's safety in numbers."

"But not always dignity," she countered. "Being

afraid interferes with my own self-esteem. I don't see myself as being a cowardly person," she told him.

He nodded. He could see where she was coming from. As they talked, he forced himself to start making his way to the front door. Otherwise, he wasn't going to leave, no matter what she decided.

"Maybe," he agreed, "but at least you'll be alive to have those self-esteem issues."

She stopped for a moment to look at him, *really* look at him. "Are you always this pessimistic?"

"I'm not a pessimist," Zane corrected, "I'm a realist."

"What you are is depressing," she countered sadly. "We're really going to have to work on changing that about you."

He found her choice of pronouns interesting because there was no "we." Moreover, there were no plans for them to evolve to that particular state. It would be better for everyone if he just pulled back so no misunderstandings flared between them. What he had offered her was strictly professional, nothing more

Yeah, right, an inner voice mocked him.

"You have my card?" he asked, suddenly intent on making good his getaway.

"Yes, somewhere," she answered vaguely.

He frowned and pulled out his card. Flipping it over, he wrote down his personal cell phone number, the one that, until now, only Billy had access to. Holding it out to her, he said, "Now you have another with my cell number on it," he added.

She took it from him and glanced at the writing. She could read the numbers, but just barely. "Maybe I'll start a collection."

The frown deepened, spreading to a furrowed brow. "This is serious, Alyx."

"And this is how I deal with serious," she informed him glibly.

And it was. Alyx had always used humor as a defense mechanism, as a shield and as a way to knock off steam when she felt particularly stressed. Humor saw her through a crisis and she was grateful for it.

She placed the card right next to the phone in the living room. "Don't worry, I'll keep it right here." She patted the card for emphasis. "If Harry shows up, you'll definitely be the first person I call." The straight face she tried to maintain finally broke up and she grinned.

He wanted to tell her it wasn't funny. That he would feel better, despite her sensible argument, if she'd let him hang around, keeping watch. He couldn't do it while he was on duty, but his off hours were his own to do with as he pleased. Still, he knew Alyx needed to do what she felt she had to. It wasn't up to him to force her into agreeing.

Besides, more than likely, Harry *was* nowhere to be found. They had an APB out on him covering the state, but his suspicions were that Harry was halfway across the country or into Mexico by now.

"See that I am the first person you call," he told her gruffly. With that, he started to cross the living room to the front door.

"Zane?" she called after him.

He stopped to glance over his shoulder. "Yes?"

Her smile was soft this time, and all the more gut-twisting for it. "Thanks for worrying."

When he found his tongue, Zane started to protest that he wasn't worrying, that it was his job to make sure the citizens of this city were safe and she was a citizen. But he had a feeling she could see through that, too.

So instead he just mumbled "Yeah" and continued on his way out.

She stopped him dead in his tracks with a quick, fleeting kiss. Just the barest contact of lips touching lips, hers in a smile, his not. A mystifying tidal wave of hunger rose within him.

He could feel himself weakening. Wanting to give in. To test the waters and the boundaries of this situation and *really* kiss her back. But doing so would be out of the box for him, not to mention bordering on harassment. He couldn't take advantage of the situation—or of her, no matter what she might protest to the contrary about being the master of her own fate. He knew better than anyone that people could be manipulated into doing things. Into being made to think, for a little while, that what was happening was by their choice or that it was somehow their fault.

Zane forced himself to step back from her, despite the fact he wanted to remain just where he was, becoming familiar with every aspect of this woman who stirred him.

"Call me if you remember something. Or if you need me."

Or just because you want to call me, he added silently.

Turning on his heel, Zane left. Before he couldn't.

Tonight, Alyx thought, would have been a good time for one of her cousins to drop in and avail themselves of one of the two other bedrooms in the apartment. But even as she mentally crossed her fingers, no one came by.

When the phone rang, she all but leaped on it. The silence was getting to her. "Hello?"

"It's your fault," the voice on the other end of the line rumbled. "It's your fault she's dead."

McBride. Was he close by? Unable to help herself, she looked around, even though she knew he couldn't be *that* close. "The police are looking for you," she said, sounding braver than she felt.

"They'll never find me," he said with confidence. "But I'll find you," he promised malevolently. "There's no place for you to hide."

With that, the line went dead.

Poor choice of words, she thought, hanging up. McBride was playing mind games, trying to scare her. Well, she wouldn't give him the satisfaction.

She also wasn't going to call Zane. He'd be over in a heartbeat, but he had enough to do without adding bodyguard to his duties.

She checked the chain at the door, then wedged a chair beneath the doorknob. Better safe than sorry, she told herself.

She spent the next hour trying to get to sleep. Of course, she failed. Her mind was just too keyed up to let her rest. Especially after McBride's phone call.

Giving up, Alyx abandoned tossing and turning and twisting her sheets and got out of bed.

The night stretched out long and dark before her. She thought of turning on the TV more for company than anything else, but there wasn't anything interesting to watch at this hour.

She decided to do a little internet surfing. There was always an endless supply of medical updates to wade through. Because she couldn't sleep, she might as well be productive. If nothing else, she thought with a suppressed smile, reading the various reports might succeed in putting her to sleep.

Walking into the third bedroom, which had been partially converted into a study, she turned on the computer and sat down. The machine hummed to life, its monitor slowly opening up like a huge, sleepy eye that blinked and focused before becoming fully alert.

As the first order of business, she opened up her in-box, then spent the next half hour deleting mail that promised her everything from doubling her bank account to enabling her to find her one true love if only she'd fill out the form on the next screen.

You'd think, she mused as her finger kept pushing

the delete button, that the people who sent out these annoying emails would get the hint when she didn't answer. Apparently not.

She pared down her emails from 320 to 85, then, finally satisfied, she felt free to surf the internet. But rather than look up the medical articles, she looked up Harry McBride. Who knew what she'd find? He and Abby hadn't been here that long. Maybe they'd lived in a smaller city before this. Hometown papers sometimes listed crimes that had been committed during the week. What if they'd moved because he'd made the papers for turning his wife into a punching bag?

The moment she typed in Harry's name, an ad popped up, telling her that for a nominal sum, she could find out everything there was to know about the eight Harry McBrides who were listed in response to her search.

The sum quoted wasn't anything that would break the weekly allotment she allowed herself.

She debated for a moment, then told herself that if she came up empty via the regular route, she'd fall back on this.

Getting rid of the ad, she found more than a handful of hits. Holding her breath, she opened up the first. It was a short article in the *Albuquerque Express,* dated four years ago. It named Harry McBride as a "person of interest" in his wife's mysterious disappearance. It seemed that no one could locate her and now her husband also had gone missing.

Alyx's mouth went dry as she continued to read. It

wasn't Abby they were talking about. It was someone named Sara.

Alyx hit "print" as she went to the next article on the list, which was another article from the New Mexico newspaper. The third hit on the list was from a Seattle newspaper, a thumbnail article in the obituary section. Robin Wales McBride, 24, had drowned in a boating accident. She was survived by her grieving husband, Harry McBride.

"God damn it," she murmured under her breath, not fully aware that she was saying this out loud, "he's killing them."

There were more.

Alyx's heart began to hammer in her chest. She printed that article next, then the others she came across. In total she connected McBride to four wives, not counting Abby. Four wives in four different states. Four wives with two things in common. They'd all been married to Harry McBride and they all died young.

Returning to the first name she'd come across, she typed in "Robin Wales McBride" to see if there was anything else on the woman. There was and it made her ill. Two years after the last article naming the vanishing Harry McBride as a possible person of interest, hikers had come across a badly decomposed body in the woods. An exceptionally diligent medical examiner had matched Robin's dental records to that of the charred victim. Cause of death couldn't be pinned down because of the decomposition.

That was all she could find. Who knew how many

more wives Harry had disposed of? "Abby's going to be your last," Alyx vowed.

Leaning back in the chair, she felt excitement race through her. This was big. Because these occurrences were scattered across several different states during different time periods, no one had bothered connecting them. Until now.

A wave of excitement akin to electricity went through her. This guy—there was no doubt in her mind—was a psychopath.

A psychopath.

The phrase echoed in her brain with mounting horror. There was no other name for him.

Alyx let out a long, shaky breath, trying to pull herself together. This was big, very big. She looked at her watch. It was two in the morning. She had to be at work, bright eyed and bushy tailed, in less than six hours.

But there was no way that she would sleep, at least not until she was able to share this with Zane.

Alyx hurried out to the living room. Where had she put his card? her brain demanded as she tried to backtrack her steps earlier this evening. And then she remembered.

She picked his card up from the table in the living room, then stood and regarded the number written there, waffling, for exactly one minute.

"He said to call if I remembered something," she said out loud, as if to talk herself into doing what she desperately wanted to do. This wasn't remembering something, but it was definitely "something" with a capital "S."

Taking a deep breath, holding his card, she pressed the keyboard on her portable telephone. She waited for the phone to ring.

When it did, she half expected to be kicked into voicemail.

When she heard his deep, baritone voice, she realized with relief that she'd gotten the man, not the recording. Thank God for small favors.

She was both surprised and relieved that he didn't sound sleepy. "Zane," she cried, "it's Alyx."

"Alyx." His voice was sharp, alert. "What's wrong? Is McBride trying to break in?"

Guilt slashed through her. She hadn't meant to worry him. "No, no, he's not here," Alyx assured him quickly, then added even more quickly, "But I think I just found something."

"Found something?" he questioned. "What do you mean? Found where?" he asked.

Her tongue was getting tangled. She wished she could get this out in a more orderly fashion. She was usually a lot calmer than this. But as it was, she was all but blurting things out.

"On the internet," she told him. "I found it on the internet. There are all sorts of articles about McBride. He's—"

"Hold it," Zane instructed. "Take it from the top. From the beginning," he stressed.

He was right, she had to be more coherent here. "I

couldn't sleep so I decided to see if I could find anything out about Abby's husband."

For a second, she heard nothing but silence on the other end. About to continue, she suddenly heard Zane say, "You found out that Abby might not be the first wife he's suspected of killing."

Stunned, she could only ask, "How did you—"

"I did a little digging of my own tonight. I had his name and as much of what seemed like an MO put into the national database that we have at the station," he told her.

Because of her cousins' husbands, Alyx thought that only detectives had access to those kinds of databases. Detective and hackers and Zane definitely didn't strike her as being a closet geek.

"You did?" she asked, trying not to sound as if she was skeptical. "Personally?"

"Let's just say I have access to someone who could do that," he answered evasively.

There was no need to tell her about the hacker he hadn't busted in exchange for the teenager's word that he would go straight—and the promise of being able to tap into the teen's vast abilities on occasions when he needed to investigate something that had no other visible avenue of information.

"This guy," Zane continued, "isn't just a wife abuser. That's just one aspect of this worthless piece of garbage's bag of tricks. He was 'a person of interest' in the death of every single wife he's had. From what I can see, in each case, there's no mention made of any previous marriages. No one made the connection. He's beginning to really look like a psychopath and maybe even a serial killer." He paused for a minute, letting his words sink in. "You know what this means, don't you?"

Alyx wasn't certain that they were on the same wavelength. "What?"

His answer surprised her. "That you're not responsible for Abby's death. One way or another, this bastard would have killed her. It was only a matter of time. From all indications, he doesn't stay married for very long."

"He wouldn't have gotten to kill her if I had been able to convince her to leave him." But she hadn't thought that it was her place to even try.

From his experience, on the force and off, most people would have taken the absolution he'd offered and just run with it.

But she hadn't.

She was definitely a woman who marched to her own drummer. He liked that.

Maybe a little too much. And that, more than the prospect of an armed gunman hiding in the shadows, made him nervous.

Chapter 11

"She wouldn't have listened," Zane assured Alyx after a beat had passed. He focused on the case before them and not on his personal reaction to the woman on the other end of the phone. "Women who allow themselves to be victims, to be abused because somehow they believe they deserve to be treated so badly and no better. They don't usually abandon the man they think they love."

Again, he paused for a moment, thinking. His concern got the better of him and came to the foreground. "Listen, I think it really might not be a bad idea for me to hang around you for a bit when I'm off duty. At least for a few days, to make sure that this dirtbag doesn't suddenly decide to pay you a visit. In his mind, he might see you as being instrumental in changing the course of his life. Men like McBride like to call all the shots, not be surprised by a curveball someone throws their way."

There was no question in Zane's mind that the missing "suspect" in Abby McBride's murder was a control freak of the first degree. Even if he didn't turn out to be a serial killer, as other evidence of his past dealings seemed to indicate, obsessively controlling personalities made for dangerous acquaintances. And could be twice as dangerous when crossed.

"And I threw him a 'curveball'?" Alyx questioned. "How?"

"You got the police involved. You got his temper to flare faster and he took it out on the first person who irritated him—his wife." The tone of his voice shifted as he brought the receiver closer to him. Alyx felt another warm shiver slide down her spine even as she tried to ignore it. "In either case, he might want to pay you back."

Alyx refused to let her mind go there. "I'll be fine," she told him, cutting Zane off and simultaneously banking down the physical responses to him she was experiencing. Or trying to. "I'm not alone that much. My cousins make a habit of dropping by. And while the idea of having a guardian angel with a gun hovering around does sound interesting, there's really no need. You have more than enough to do. Your off-duty hours should be just that—off duty."

"Your choice," Zane responded, backing off. "Well, good night."

"Good night," she said, but the line was dead already. She stared at it for a moment, a little stunned that he'd been convinced *that* fast.

Had she hurt his feelings, turning him down so quickly?

Off the top of her head she would have said that the patrolman didn't have any feelings, at least that was the way he struck her. She couldn't shake the impression that she had managed to unintentionally step on his toes—and his ego.

She replaced the receiver into the cradle and rose to her feet. Walking into the kitchen, Alyx put on a pot of coffee. It promised to be a *very* long night with no sleep.

It wasn't that she wouldn't have liked having Zane around or even that she wouldn't have felt better with him here. The answer to both was a resounding "yes." God knows he had managed to spook her a little talking about McBride's desire for revenge. Most likely, she wasn't going to sleep too well not just tonight but for the next six months or so.

Given her active imagination, she would magnify every noise she heard—or thought she heard—and she'd be seeing McBride hiding in all the shadows. But, admittedly, having Zane around scared her even more. Because the patrolman attracted her. Strongly.

She could so easily see herself falling for him, falling for the man with his flat abdomen, his hard body and his beautiful, beautiful stormy-blue eyes. They might not be as expressive as she would have liked, but she could still see herself getting lost in them with just a glance.

And as for his smile—when he smiled—well, that sent her body temperature into the next bracket of ten. She had a pretty good hunch that all these feelings would be one-sided and she really didn't need any additional frustrations right now. Just having to interact with the doctor from hell was enough for her to deal with. Having her emotions trapped in a shark cage by this man whose very manner made it clear that he was a loner and intended to remain that way was just asking for trouble.

And that was one thing she never asked for.

It had been raining all day long, coming down as if God had left the faucet on. At noon, when she made a mad dash across the street to pick up sandwiches for herself and a couple of the people on duty with her, Alyx was fairly certain that she'd seen a man with a flowing white beard collecting two of everything.

The effect of the humidity that came along with the rain was almost overpowering. By the end of the day, that oppressive air had managed to penetrate absolutely everything—especially the parking structure. The heavy air made it particularly difficult to drag herself through the structure at the end of her exceptionally long day.

Somehow she'd allowed herself to take on a second shift because Eloise had called in sick. In her heart, she knew the ER resident's young daughter was the sick one, but she'd agreed to take the doctor's shift.

Now she was finally going home. And none too soon. She wasn't sure just how much energy she had left.

Even putting one foot in front of the other was challenging. Mentally, she started counting the steps, trying to take her mind off the fact that the parking structure was almost empty.

The rain had abated, but the humidity had not. It expanded, pressing down everything in its path. If she didn't know better, she would have said that the air coming into her lungs was actually solid. At least it felt that way.

As she made her way through the parking structure, Alyx thought she heard something behind her.

Footsteps?

But when she turned around, there was no one around. From what she could see when she scanned the area, she seemed to be alone. The operative word here being "seemed."

"You're letting your imagination run away with you," she upbraided herself in a hushed whisper.

Nevertheless, Alyx forced herself to pick up her pace and walk faster. Her footsteps echoed back at her. Or at least she *thought* those were her footsteps. Try as she might, she couldn't shake the feeling that she was being followed.

When she turned the corner on the second level of the structure—still with no one else in sight—Alyx made herself as small as possible. Hiding in the shadows, she raised her umbrella over her head, holding it as if it was a bat. It wasn't much of a weapon but better than nothing. If she had to, she could run fast right after she struck a blow.

And she could scream. She didn't see anyone around, but her scream could summon an army. Her sisters always complained that her voice was exceptionally loud and carried for blocks.

Having felt leaden just a few moments ago, she was now alert and ready to fight. Adrenaline was firing through her veins in double-time.

She heard it again. She was right. Those *were* footsteps behind her.

Her heart was set to explode out of her chest as she heard the footsteps coming closer.

He was almost on top of her.

With a guttural yell, Alyx swung the weapon in her hands, connecting hard just as the man shadowing her steps came around the corner where she was hiding.

She dropped the umbrella the second she saw him. But it was too late, she had already made contact, hitting his shoulder. The only thing she managed to do was divert the blow, which would have connected with his head had she not quickly lowered her arms.

Still, she knew that it had been a hard blow despite the fact that he swallowed his cry of pain. The resulting muffled groan told her all she needed to know. That, and she had put most of her weight into the swing. She'd hurt him. The *wrong* him.

"Zane!" she cried, horrified at what could have just happened. He grabbed his shoulder, then let his hand drop, but he wasn't fooling her. She'd hurt him. The question was, how much? "Why are you following me?"

Pain radiated out up into his neck and down along his arm.

"To protect you," he answered, trying to modulate his voice so that the pain would not show through and give him away. For such a small woman, he marveled at the amount of power she had in those arms. "Obviously you don't need as much protecting as I thought. Right now, I'm beginning to think that McBride would lose in any sort of a confrontation with you." He realized that he was unconsciously rubbing his shoulder and let his hand drop to his side again. He glanced down on the ground to make sure she'd used an umbrella and not a tire iron. "Where the hell did you learn to swing like that?"

"I used to play baseball with the neighborhood boys when I was growing up in Chicago," she told him. Back then, it was a matter of pride not to let the boys show her up. She used to practice every chance she got, tossing up a ball and hitting it, then having one of her sisters go running after it. It took her an entire summer, but she got very, very good at power hitting.

He laughed shortly. "I would have hated to be in the outfield when you came up to bat."

Alyx pressed her lips together as guilt wafted through her. "I'm so sorry. But I didn't know it was you. I thought…" She let her voice trail off for a moment, then raised her eyes to his face. "You spooked me, saying what you did about McBride coming after me."

He hadn't wanted to scare her, but he did want her to be aware of what could happen. "Better safe than sorry, although I'm going to have to revise my image of you being this helpless, delicate damsel in distress."

"There's something else."

He looked at her, alert, his pain temporarily forgotten. "What?"

"McBride called me. He said it was my fault his wife was dead and that he was coming after me."

"Damn it, why didn't you lead with that?" Zane demanded. "You should have called me right away."

"I did—after I found something substantial to give you. I can take care of myself," she pointed out.

"Yeah." He knew there was no point in arguing with her. He'd never win.

Zane rotated his shoulder and sharp blades of pain raced through his arm and back up his neck. He thought he'd masked the pain, but the look on her face told him he'd failed to keep it entirely to himself.

She took hold of his other arm, ready to turn him around. "Why don't we go back to the hospital and I'll just—"

He held his ground. "That's all right. It's not broken. I'm just going to have one hell of a black-and-blue mark on it for a while." He shrugged, then winced before the motion was complete. "Or longer," he added.

"Vitamin C," she said quickly, interjecting her words into his before he had a chance to finish. He raised an eyebrow and she explained, "If you take a lot of vitamin

C over the course of the day, it helps keep the bruising to a minimum."

He supposed that made sense—except for the doling out part. "Why can't I just take whatever the dose is all at once and be done with it?"

"Because your body just takes what it needs and lets the rest just pass right through." What if she hadn't curtailed her swing at the last minute? What if she'd followed through and hit his head? He'd be lying at her feet, unconscious or much worse. The thought shook her up. "Look, if you won't go to the hospital, why don't you come home with me and let me take a look at it? I can at least make the swelling go down."

That coincided with his original suggestion to hang around her for a while to make sure that McBride didn't show up and hurt her.

"Sounds like a plan to me," he agreed and, by the expression on his face, Alyx saw that she had played right into his hands.

But she couldn't very well rescind the offer now that she'd extended it. Besides, she had to admit that having someone with her *did* make her feel better. Coming home to an empty apartment wasn't exactly appealing right now.

"Where're you parked?" he asked. When she pointed out the spot, he nodded. "You get in your car and stay right there. I'll just get mine and follow you to your place."

"Can you drive?" she asked, concerned. She nodded at his arm.

"I've driven with a bullet hole in my arm. I can drive," he assured her. Zane began walking away, then stopped abruptly. He'd forgotten to give her one vital piece of information. "By the way, it's a Honda Accord."

Alyx didn't understand. She shook her head. "What is?"

"My car." And then the corners of Zane's mouth curved ever so slightly. He'd guessed right. From her expression, he could tell that she'd assumed he was driving the black and white. "They won't let me take the squad car home."

"Right. Of course they wouldn't." Feeling a little foolish, Alyx turned on her heel and hurried off to her car. Unlocking it, she got in to wait for his return.

She still couldn't shake the feeling that she was being watched, but that, she was now ready to admit, was just her paranoia.

God, how could he have gotten even better looking since the last time? Was it even humanly possible?

The moment they'd walked through her doorway and shut the door behind them, Alyx had turned around and insisted that he remove his shirt.

"There's no reason for you to play doctor, Doc. It's just a welt at best."

"I'll be the judge of that. Now take off your shirt," she'd told him.

When he began to unbutton his shirt, she'd had to admit to herself that her stomach had tightened and her body temperature had once again gone up. What was the effect this man had over her?

His upper torso was as perfect as any she had ever seen. More. The only thing that kept it from being beyond perfection was that he had a total of three scars. One on his chest, one on his shoulder and the last on his back. But with him, it only added to the image, not detracted from it.

Even the red welt she'd awarded him didn't take away from the aura he created.

She made him wait while she hurried off to the bathroom to fetch a few things from the medicine cabinet. When she returned, she was mixing a pale pink paste in what looked like a tea cup.

"You have no idea how close you came to my hitting your head," she told him, contrition echoing in every syllable. "I pulled my swing at the last minute when I saw that it was you."

"Good thing they have got decent lighting in the garage," he cracked dryly, watching her stir the concoction.

The small sound of dismay escaped her lips as she looked at the red, angry welt on his shoulder. If possible, it looked even worse now than it had when she'd made him take his shirt off.

"I am so, so sorry," she told him, a fresh wave of guilt washing over her. "What can I do to make it up to you?"

He had his answer all ready for her. "Let me play

bodyguard for a few days when I'm off duty and we'll call it even."

She didn't see how that absolved her, but she wasn't about to argue. "You should have told me that you were going to shadow me."

"I did," he reminded her, "And you vetoed it. I rely a lot on gut instincts, and mine told me you needed protecting." He glanced at the welt and a smile played on his lips. "My gut instincts aren't always a hundred percent right."

She laughed then and began to apply the salve to his arm with slow, careful strokes. "I could have told you that."

The salve felt cool against his skin. Cool and oddly soothing. He raised his eyes to her face. "That feels good. What is it?"

"Just something I came up with," she said, shrugging off any further explanation. She was fairly certain that he wouldn't have wanted to know what was really in the mixture. "Sometimes the homemade remedies are the best," she told him. Putting down the cup, she began to work the salve into his skin, her long fingers gliding along his shoulder in small, even strokes.

She became aware of every breath he took as she worked.

"Smells good," he told her, raising his eyes to her face.

Damn, there went her heartbeat again, locking into double-time. "Just a little vanilla added to cover up the actual—"

"I meant you," he said. His voice was low, his words all but pulsating on her skin. His eyes lingered on hers. "You smell nice. Like the way home should," he heard himself say and wondered where in God's name that had come from. Home for him had become more of an idea, a concept, not a place. What was he doing, talking about this to her? To anyone?

He sat on a stool while she worked over the area between his shoulder and biceps. Her face, she realized too late, was barely inches away from his, so close she could feel his breath travel along her skin.

So close that, she was certain, he could feel hers along his.

Her pulse quickened even more. She didn't know why the thought of their breaths touching one another aroused her, but it did.

So much so that her heart suddenly hammered harder now than in the parking structure when she thought she was in danger. Maybe this was a kind of danger, too. A different kind. One where, if she wasn't careful, she could easily lose her footing. Not to mention other things.

Her heart wasn't letting up. It now pounded so hard she was afraid it might come right out of her chest and fall at his feet like an offering.

He turned a fraction of an inch on the stool, coming even closer to her, closer than a prayer at midnight.

Her scalp tingled in anticipation as Zane threaded his fingers through her hair, gently framing her face.

"What…what are you doing?" she asked, her mouth so dry she was amazed that the words even emerged.

"Shh," he whispered. "I'm better at showing than explaining."

And then the next moment, he was doing just that. Showing her. Showing Alyx just what being so close to her had done to him. It had made her completely and utterly impossible for him to resist. He'd struggled with the onslaught of urges that marched through him. He'd struggled with them for as long as he could, but then he'd seen the flash of desire in her eyes and known that he was bound to let this happen.

To kiss her again.

Not just to kiss her, but take it as far as she would allow. Everything inside of him demanded it. Begged for it.

And made him feel that his drawing even a breath tomorrow hinged on if he could have her tonight.

If she turned him down tonight, he would back away no matter how great the need. But he was fairly certain that in doing so, in keeping to his code, he would self-destruct. Wanting her as much as he did right now would be his undoing because, with nothing to feed on, the hunger would turn on him and, within a very short time, completely destroy him.

But she didn't turn him down.

And everything within him rejoiced.

Chapter 12

Over and over again, his mouth slanted over Alyx's, kissing her, drawing sustenance from her.

The more he kissed her, the more he wanted to kiss her.

To touch her.

To have her.

It was like a fever in the blood that he was powerless to stop.

Zane realized that he wasn't the master of this situation. She was. He found himself completely overwhelmed with the taste, the feel, the very scent of her. It permeated all his senses until only she remained in his world—a frightening concept if he allowed himself to think about it.

So he didn't.

He stopped thinking at all.

His lips still sealed to hers, Zane pulled her onto his lap, his arms locking around her despite the salvo of pain that shot through the shoulder she had smashed the umbrella against. The pain was a small price to pay for having her so near now.

But even as he kissed Alyx, from somewhere deep within the shadows of his soul, a sliver of common sense burrowed its way to the surface through the fire and the passion. He was concerned about her safety. If he went on to make love with her, the way he ached to, she might think that his concern was all a ruse just to get to this point, to make love with her. Then, once things calmed down, she would send him away,

He couldn't let that happen.

So, with a silent, anguished cry of deprivation that echoed to the depths of his soul, Zane forced himself to stop kissing her and draw his head back. It was excruciatingly hard.

Stunned, caught off guard and dealing with a monumental feeling of bereavement, Alyx blinked. She struggled to erase the fog enshrouding her brain.

Why?

"Is something wrong?" she asked in a low, hoarse voice overflowing with emotion.

"Nothing's wrong." In his opinion, no moment had been more perfect, which, he had to admit, scared him. Perfection didn't exist in the real world.

"Then why did you suddenly stop?" she asked.

He didn't know just how long he could remain noble if she pushed. "I didn't want you getting the wrong impression."

The quizzical look did not leave her eyes. "About what?"

All right, so she needed it spelled out for her. He could do that—as long as he didn't look into her eyes. If he did, he'd be trapped there, a willing prisoner. "I didn't want you thinking that I'd said what I had about protecting you just to get you into bed."

Alyx smiled then, a soft, radiant smile that damn near punched him in the gut. He could hardly catch his breath.

The fact that he was concerned about what she thought touched her. Her smile widened as she remained on his lap. "Don't worry, Zane, I don't see you as being that devious."

He frowned slightly, a furrow forming between his eyebrows. "Was that an insult?"

She laughed, shaking her head. "No, that was a compliment about your honesty. You're not the type to play games. You don't make up lies just to get what you want. That's not how you think," she told him with a certainty that amazed him. "That's what makes this all so right. You won't say things to string me along. It's a matter of what I see is what I get," she told him in a barely audible voice, her eyes on his.

She seemed to peer into his soul. Suddenly, Zane felt like the one being seduced. And he had to admit, he rather enjoyed that.

Pulling Alyx closer to him, he was about to kiss her again. But instead, he found himself kissing her raised fingers, which she held up between his lips and hers. It was his turn to be puzzled.

"I don't want you hurting your shoulder," she explained.

"Don't worry, my shoulder has very little to do with this," he assured her.

Before Alyx could say anything else, his lips were on hers again, sealing in her words. At the same time, the very feel of his lips on hers released all her passions and urges.

In less than a moment, the pent-up feelings she had exploded, bathing the world around her with breathtaking colors. Even before they went any further, before his lips left hers to explore the rest of her, Alyx knew in her heart that she had never experienced this before.

She couldn't wait.

Rising from the stool, he held her against him, thrilling at the outline of her body melding into his. Bending into him as if the two of them were already one. Eagerness reared within him, desperate to make her his, to bring the softly whispered promise echoing in his head like a formless shadow into fruition.

With his lips still sealed to hers, Zane slowly ran his hands up and down along her torso, his fingers and palms worshiping all the tempting curves that comprised her body.

He tasted rather than heard the moan that escaped

her lips and it fanned the flames of his excitement to the point that it became very, very hard to rein himself in, to go slow instead of steamroll ahead.

But he managed.

Managed because this was their first time and it would leave a lasting impression on her. He wanted Alyx to look back on this moment with fondness. And if this was their only time together—and who knew what tomorrow would bring—then Zane wanted it to really matter.

To be the best that he could give her.

Trying to school himself to go slow, he still wound up peeling away her clothes to the same tempo that she stripped away his. Her pullover electric-blue top hit the floor a beat before his pullover gray polo suffered the same fate.

A flurry of fabric showered down on the variegated gray rug beneath their feet until, just like that, there were no physical barriers left. Mental barriers went next, quickly vanquished in the same manner as needs trumped fears.

His hands caressed her, his fingertips sculpting her form and making love to every inch of her a beat after his eyes did.

Zane drew her down onto the sofa, unable to go any further. His desires had gotten the better of him, demanding their due.

He bestowed his own form of worship on her, using his lips, his teeth, his tongue to sample, to anoint and then, just as quickly, to completely possess every single inch of her warm, pliant flesh.

She'd fantasized about this but had never truly believed that it could be like this. That lovemaking could be so fiery, so prolonged, so exquisite. To her, always before, the act had disappointed her.

But not this time.

Zane brought every single fiber of her to life. Not only to life, but his very artful touch made parts of her vibrate so hard she didn't think they would ever settle down again. She didn't want them to.

His questing mouth did unbelievable things. Made her feel the way she had always dreamed. The explosions were wondrous.

Alyx arched and bucked, as one climax after another flowered into a shower of stars and fireworks to the point that she was soon completely breathless and exhausted.

Who knew it could be like this? That it wasn't just a single, swift moment in time, but what felt like an eternity?

If this was a dream, she never wanted to wake up again.

And then, she was aware of Zane's body slowly sliding up along hers. Aware of her legs being gently urged apart with his knee. It suddenly registered that her eyes were shut. Forcing them open, she found herself looking into his face.

A face that took her breath away all over again— because there was an expression of tenderness she had never witnessed before. It transformed the hard, rigid lines of Zane's solemn face, making him look almost boyish.

It was probably her imagination, but she still clung to it. Clung to the impression it cast.

Her heart swelled. If she hadn't known better, she would have said that was the moment that she fell in love with him.

Zane laced his fingers through hers, forming a union a heartbeat before he joined her in the ultimate one. Anticipation rushing in her veins, Alyx raised her hips to him in a silent invitation.

And then he entered her.

The final dance began as her hips sealed to his and the ensuing rhythm seized them both.

The tempo went faster and faster until, several heartbeats later, his arms tightening around her, they reached the apex together.

His heart slammed against hers. She could feel her own mimicking its accelerated tempo. It heightened the experience even more. She found herself holding on to him for dear life, bracing herself for the spiraling descent that had to follow even as she fervently prayed that it wouldn't.

Alyx held her breath, as if that could somehow hold the final moments in abeyance a second longer.

But she knew it couldn't.

Alyx felt Zane relax against her. His embrace loosened, and a sadness began to envelop her.

The next second, rather than retreating into his own

world the way she fully expected him to, Zane raised himself up on his elbows to look down into her face.

"Did I hurt you?" he asked.

Concern. He was showing concern. *After* the fact, when he had nothing to gain.

She liked that.

Her mouth curved as humor filled her eyes. "I'll let you know when I can feel my body again. How's your shoulder?" Her eyes shifted toward that part of his anatomy, the doctor pushing aside the lover.

"What shoulder?"

She laughed at that and the sound rippled between them like a feathery tickle, touching them both.

Unable to help himself, Zane stole a kiss from her as if they hadn't just made love, but were two innocents on the brink of discovering the soft, fresh petals of first love.

About to laugh again, the sound faded away in her throat as she looked up at Zane and saw that his expression had turned serious again. At the same moment, she became aware of the growing hardness of his body as it continued to press against hers.

Alyx looped her arms around his neck and whispered softly, "I'm ready if you are."

He shouldn't be.

He never had been before. Until now, the act of lovemaking had always been a once-only process, followed by a restless peacefulness. That was a complete contradiction in terms, he knew, but so was most of his life. He was a nonconformist who conformed to rules because he wanted to be a cop rather than a criminal. Because of who and what he was, those were the only two options in his life.

He chose being a cop because it brought freedom with it.

But with this strange, innocent but worldly woman who was all things at once, he found himself ready to make love again in what amounted to a heartbeat.

"Maybe we should notify the AMA," he whispered, lightly touching her lips with his own after he uttered each word.

Her body already vibrated in anticipation and her heart had spontaneously launched into double-time, as both hungrily awaited more.

"About?" she breathed.

He kissed her eyelids, her brow, the hollow of her cheeks. "About the transformation you brought about in me."

"Not yet," she said with effort—it was difficult to talk when she felt as if her heart was lodged in her throat. "We have to test and re-test the theory a hundred times or so before we can really say that our findings are justified."

His smile, she noticed, included his eyes for the first time since she'd met him. Why did that prompt rays of sunshine to fill her being?

"I'm game if you are," he told her.

Her chest rubbed against his as she drew in a breath. Her body tingled in response. "More than game," she assured him, her voice low, then repeated the words with feeling in case he hadn't heard her the first time. "More than game."

It was the last thing Alyx said for a long time to come.

The desire to flee, which always followed once the act was over, didn't even register. Another new experience for him.

Their lovemaking had taken them from her living room to her bedroom, each location giving way to more heated couplings between them. After they were both completely and utterly exhausted, Zane fell asleep holding her in his arms.

Consequently, he spent the night in her bed, something else that, as a rule, he never did. He didn't sleep— literally sleep—with anyone. He slept alone. He always had, valuing his independence and his solitude after the act of lovemaking was over.

But this time, he wasn't eager to leave. Not only not eager, but actually loathed to leave. He could have shrugged it off and told himself that he had only promised to protect her. But that would have been a lie and he never lied, especially not to himself.

His promise to hang around and watch over her could have easily been fulfilled by his remaining on the sofa in the living room. That, after all, was what he'd initially told her he intended to do.

But he'd remained in her bed. Remained there because he'd *wanted* to. He'd wanted to watch her sleep, to feel her breath against his skin as she gently, rhythmically breathed in and out beside him. He'd wanted to just drink in everything about this witch who'd cast a spell over him.

He was the first one to admit that life was short and unstable. Tomorrow might bring about an emotional earthquake that would change absolutely everything. So he wanted to enjoy, to savor, this tiny island of happiness he'd been washed onto before he was once again swept out to sea.

While his feelings scared the hell out of him, he needed to get dressed and go back on patrol. All of life's harsh realities were back in play.

She dreamed she'd gone to paradise. To a place where life was perfect and always would be.

But even as she dreamed it, Alyx was aware of her dreaming. Because, amid all the optimism, she was still a realist and knew that nothing was ever perfect—at least not for long. The best that she could possibly hope for was that she might feel this same passion and happiness in the future.

But even in her dream, she understood that life was not a straight line. It fluctuated without rhyme or reason. The thought disturbed her enough to rouse her from the depths of sleep and leave her on the beach with dawn breaking.

With extreme reluctance, her moment passed, Alyx opened her eyes. His face was the first thing she saw. She smiled in greeting until her brain kicked in. Zane looked at her.

"Oh God, don't look at me," she cried. Grabbing the sheet, she pulled it up over her head. Hiding.

Laughing, Zane tugged at the sheet, thinking to bring it down again. He was surprised that it took more force than he'd expected.

"Why? Why can't I look at you?" he asked, managing to tug it down.

Alyx pulled it back up again. "Because I look terrible."

"Well then 'terrible' has a brand new definition," he informed her, a ribbon of affection lacing itself through his voice.

With a mighty tug, he pulled the sheet out of her hands, throwing it aside. Before she could protest, he leaned into her and pressed a kiss against her throat, then one each to her breasts. His breath caressed her skin, heating it.

"Oh, don't start," she pleaded. "We'll be late. *I'll* be late," she emphasized, hoping to get him to stop. Because she had absolutely no defenses against him. Certainly common sense played no part here either. Not when her own body rebelled against her already.

Zane drew his head back just enough to be able to raise his eyes beguilingly to hers. He was the embodiment of temptation.

"You really want me to stop?" he asked, his warm breath making her belly tighten hard with renewed anticipation.

Alyx's skin quivered in response and she sunk into

the promise of what was to come. Just like that, she surrendered.

"Hell, no. Don't you dare stop," she ordered him, sliding back down flat against the bed and into Zane's kiss.

Chapter 13

Almost a month later, Zane told himself that he could walk away at any time.

Which is why he didn't.

Because the option was open to him, leaving him free to enjoy her and the sweet, optimistic innocence she generated wherever she went. The moment it seemed as if there was no turning back for him, he would.

He had to.

It was as simple as that.

He didn't believe in happy endings, and life was filled with enough grief without opening himself to more. He had only to remember his parents to reinforce his beliefs. Once upon a time, he'd thought they were happy, too.

For the time being, he'd continue on this path. After

all, he had to keep Alyx safe and make sure that the man he believed beat his wife to death wouldn't do the same to Alyx. Although, he had to admit, the possibility of that happening seemed less and less likely. Harry McBride, for all intents and purposes, appeared to have disappeared off the face of the earth five seconds after he'd emptied out the joint bank account he and his late wife had shared. The one that held the fruits of her labors because, from everything that he and the detective working the case had discerned, the last time McBride was employed was before he and Abby were married. And that was eighteen months ago.

More than four weeks had passed since McBride had killed his wife. *Allegedly* killed his wife, Zane amended. And he had been Alyx's unofficial bodyguard for almost as long.

And her lover for the same amount of time.

Just passing through. You're just passing through, he silently reminded himself.

Exasperation chipped away at his mood as, glaring at his reflection in the mirror, he attempted once again to successfully tie the navy blue tie that hung about his neck like a deconstructed noose. He hadn't had one of those on since he couldn't remember when. First Communion? He wasn't sure. He might have worn a clip-on back then.

Maybe he should have bought one this time, he thought grudgingly. He was going with Alyx to her cousin's wedding—an event he didn't remember agreeing to attend—and those kinds of celebrations, he assumed, called for wearing uncomfortable things like jackets, crisp shirts and ties.

Finished—again—he looked at his handiwork. One end was twice as long as the other.

Who the hell had invented this useless appendage anyway? Swallowing a curse, Zane yanked the lopsided tie apart for what felt like the fifteenth time. This time, instead of beginning the process from scratch, he shoved the annoying tie into his jacket pocket.

Maybe Alyx would know how to tie a tie properly, he thought irritably.

He glanced at his watch. If he didn't get going he would be late picking her up. She hated being late. They had that in common.

Zane hurried out of his apartment.

Twenty minutes later as he drove into the bowels of her apartment building's parking structure, he realized that they had a great deal in common. And just enough differences to make things interesting—for the time being, he sternly reminded himself.

Leaving his car in guest parking, Zane hurried over to the elevator and took it up to the fifth floor. Even though he was dressed—except for the tie—and ready to go, part of him debated coming up with an excuse to bail. He could always tell her that they had tapped him for extra duty. It wasn't that unusual an occurrence.

He'd never been to a wedding before and now didn't seem like a good time to start. Especially if it made her think that he was amenable to marriage—because he wasn't. That institution would never be part of his life. If others wanted to take a chance, that was their choice. As far as he was concerned, he took enough of a risk putting on his uniform every morning.

Getting out on Alyx's floor, Zane made his way to her apartment, framing and refining the excuse he had decided to give her. He could say that the sergeant had called at the last minute, just as he was leaving. That would explain why he wore a sports jacket and dress slacks. He grew more and more pleased with his plan.

After all, he thought, pressing her doorbell, the whole point of his being around Alyx was to make sure she was safe. If he happened to enjoy himself, all the better. But if he didn't—and he knew damn well that he wouldn't at a wedding—well then he could just—

The door opened and at that exact moment, he completely lost the ability to think at all, never mind clearly.

And she was to blame.

Alyx wore a soft, bluish-gray gown that was slit almost all the way up her leg and clung to every curve along the journey. It—and she—were, quite frankly, the stuff that dreams were made of.

Erotic male dreams.

He'd seen her nude, had caressed her body and made love to her, but somehow, seeing her in the form-hugging gown, he was struck speechless. He had to remind himself to breathe—then try to remember exactly how that was done.

When he finally found his tongue, he told her, "I'm

not sure if it's legal to take you out in that. I might be breaking some kind of anti-riot law. Maybe several of them," he speculated.

His eyes washed over her as he committed every inch of her form to memory.

"You know, for a man who claims to be very plainspoken, you do know how to turn a phrase," Alyx told him with a laugh. Its timbre warmed the very bottom of his dark soul. "And just for the record," she added, smoothing down the edge of the collar he'd accidentally left up, "you clean up very nicely, too." She nodded toward the inside of the apartment. "Come in. I just have to go get my purse."

At a loss for words, Zane nodded and he followed her inside. He shoved his hands into his pockets. Which was when he remembered.

"Oh. How are you with ties?" he asked, holding aloft the one that had given him so much grief less than a half hour ago.

Alyx looked at it and shook her head. "Never had anyone to practice on," she told him honestly. She had a feeling, from the way he'd growled out the words, that he hated ties. After taking it from him, she tossed it carelessly aside onto the sofa. "Besides, I think you look very good just the way you are."

Well, that was a relief. But he didn't want to embarrass her by being the only man who showed up without a tie. "You sure I don't need to wear a tie?"

Smiling, she shook her head. "Nope. You can go any way you want to." She picked up her clutch purse and tucked it under her arm. She then threaded her other arm through his. "After all, you're doing me a favor, coming with me."

So much for begging off, he thought. But now that he had seen her, he really didn't want to. Not if it meant that she would attend the wedding looking like that. He might wind up having to guard her from more than a supposed serial killer.

Just as they left her apartment, she paused to brush her lips against his cheek. "Thank you. I really appreciate this."

Zane shrugged away her words, mumbling something unintelligible under his breath. Responding to thanks was something he had never been very good at. Now was no exception.

"So, this is being the man who is protecting you?" Josef Pulaski asked. He made no secret of looking the man standing beside his niece up and down. After a beat, satisfied, he put out his large, hamlike hand, waiting for Alyx's escort to take it.

The wedding ceremony had been beautiful and had left the family patriarch both happy and sad at the same time. Marja was the last of his daughters, and although none of the girls had actually lived at the house in Queens for a while now, marriage brought the separation home to him and made it official. The "nest" was now really empty.

During the church ceremony, his wife handed him the extra handkerchief she'd brought with her. "It is lucky then that Paulina has decided we are family after all and sent Aleksandra to us. The other girls, they will be coming too," she said with the certainty of a mother.

Josef had tried to grumble and make noises like a man who felt as if he was being put upon, but he fooled no one. He was happy about this new turn of events. All four of his nieces were coming to New York. To his wife and him, at least initially.

Uncle Josef, a retired NYPD sergeant, liked nothing better than being a father figure. Liked being needed and, although he did have a good relationship with all of his sons-in-law, being the protector of a female member of the family made him feel useful the way running his own security firm did not even begin to approximate.

And now, he thought, looking at Zane Calloway, there was another one to inspect. Another young buck who had come from nowhere to nose around his herd. A decent young buck. He had already had Leokadia's husband do a little digging into this Zane's background and, from everything Byron had found out, Zane Calloway was a very decent, honorable young man—even if he wasn't Polish.

Zane had the distinct impression that he was being x-rayed. The short, squat bull of a man who had an iron grip on his hand eyed him as if he could see clear down to his bones. Maybe he could.

Alyx came to his rescue. "Uncle Josef, no questions. You promised."

"Questions are part of talking. I am allowed to be

talking, yes?" He looked expectantly to Zane for him to agree.

Zane saw no advantage to opposing the man. "Yeah, sure." A beat passed. Zane cleared his throat. "Um, Mr. Pulaski?"

Josef raised one very expressive, shaggy, dark eyebrow in a silent query. "Yes?"

Zane indicated the undissolved union between them. "Can I have my hand back?"

Josef laughed, loosening his grip and allowing Zane to withdraw his hand. "Sorry. I was busy deciding if you are being a good man."

From out of nowhere, Magda descended on her husband and had come in time to catch the last sentence he'd uttered. "Josef!"

Josef turned around, raising his wide shoulders in an innocent shrug. "What? I should not be being honest?" he asked his wife.

"Did I pass?" Zane asked the older man, amused despite himself.

Josef nodded his head. "You are passing," the former police sergeant assured him. He gestured toward one of the tables where the bride's family was to be seated. "Now, eat or my wife will be being very unhappy. She is the one who cooked this feast," he told Zane, turning the word "cooked" into two syllables with the emphasis on the second. "And when you are finished eating, you are to be dancing with my niece," Josef instructed. There was no room for argument.

Zane lowered his head and told Alyx, "I don't dance," the moment her uncle moved away.

The orchestra her uncle had hired was tuning up. "That's okay," she assured him. "When something a little slower than a polka comes up, you can just stand there, hold me and sway. Nobody'll know the difference," she assured him.

Zane wasn't aware of the fact that he was smiling. "I can do that."

"Sway?"

"That, too. But I was thinking of holding you." That was a definite plus, he thought, both soothing and arousing.

Alyx smiled up into his eyes and he got that all-too-familiar feeling in his gut. The kind of feeling someone got at the apex of a hill just before the roller coaster plunged thirty feet down.

"I was, too," she told him. To her surprise, the orchestra played a slow, sexy song, something about young lovers everywhere. "Looks like you get to sway before you eat." With that, she took his hand and led him off to the dance floor.

Zane went reluctantly. "You sure about this?" he asked her uncertainly once she had staked out a section for the two of them.

Placing one of his hands against the small of her back and lacing the other through her own, Alyx turned her face up to his and told him, "Nothing to it," before she leaned her head against his chest and began to sway in time to the music.

He could feel her hips fitting against his own.

She was wrong.

There was definitely something to it, Zane thought. Actually, quite a lot to it. Having her pressed against him like this, with her family and a room full of strangers around, prohibiting him from acting on a squadron of feelings, exasperated and exhilarated him at the same time.

He was powerless to act, but for now, he would just enjoy it.

So he did.

And thought about later, when he could finally get her all to himself. When he could peel off her gown and just enjoy her, just pleasure her.

The thought sustained him for the next five hours.

The reception continued until well past midnight. Because it was being held in the restaurant that Magda owned, there was no cutoff period. People were encouraged to stay and only left when too tired to remain.

Because of that, there was no mass exodus. Many of the guests stayed long after the bride and groom had escaped, amid a hail of good wishes and rice—a tradition Magda insisted on—to begin their honeymoon: a trip to Hawaii, which was a gift from Josef and Magda.

During the course of the reception, Zane met the rest of Alyx's cousins and their husbands. Full of life and enthusiasm, the members of Alyx's family seemed to more than fill the room on their own, without the benefit of the rest of the wedding guests. And although he was a loner and an outsider observing the festivities and interactions, Zane had to admit that he envied Alyx this family unit.

For him at this point, "family" had been narrowed down to one brother whose whereabouts were unknown and another he rarely saw unless Billy needed money or to be bailed out—literally and otherwise. Beyond that, he didn't hear from his troubled youngest brother for months at a time. In the beginning, after their mother had died, he'd attempted to reach Billy more than once in between life-and-death calls, but that, for the most part, had been unsuccessful. Billy just went deeper into the imaginary world his drugs created for him. After a while, Zane just gave up.

The only other "family" he had comprised the men and women in blue he worked with. There was a brotherhood of sorts, a code to be honored. But he was alone.

Which suited him just fine. Every now and then, he caught himself wondering what it would be like to have his existence—the very fact of whether he lived or died—matter to someone. The way each member of their extended family seemed to matter to Josef and Magda Pulaski.

"They take a bit of getting used to," Alyx agreed, reading the pensive expression on his face as he watched her aunt and uncle on the dance floor.

Josef had finally managed to get Magda to stop being the owner of the restaurant catering the reception and just be his wife and the mother of the bride for the space of a long, romantic dance. They glided along the floor now, two people very much in love despite all the hardships and trials they had been through in their years together.

Zane inclined his head. "They're not so bad," he allowed with a shrug.

She smiled at him in response. "I'm just getting to know them myself."

Just then, Natalya leaned in between them. Her words were intended for both of them. "Don't they look cute together?" she asked, nodding at her parents. She glanced toward Zane. "Dad claims to have won several tango competitions back in Poland with Mama as his partner." There was no missing the pure affection in her voice. "They still have that magic between them after all these years."

"They're lucky," Zane commented. He thought of his own parents and many other failed relationships he'd witnessed. "Most people these days don't stay together for very long, much less have anything 'magical.'"

Sasha had come over to join them in time to hear Zane's last comment. "You sound just like my husband before he became my husband and the family got hold of him," she told Zane, then studied him for a long moment. "He's a lot happier now," she added. "Everyone says so."

Alyx's radar went up. Her family—bless 'em— seemed bent on trying to convert Zane and bring him over to their side of the rainbow. She knew the comment would only get Zane's back up. Time to get him out of the line of fire.

Picking up her purse, she rose to her feet. "We can go now if you like," she told Zane.

He laughed, amused by the timing. "I was just going to tell you that we could stay a little while longer if you wanted to."

She did, but for practical reasons—and to spare him—she needed to get going.

"I'm on call tomorrow," she told him, then glanced at her watch. It was past midnight. "I mean I'm on call today. I'd better try and get some rest. I'm going to need it to do battle with the Wicked Witch of the West."

Sasha's ears perked up. "You mean Gloria Furst? The chief resident from hell?" she asked, turning around to face her cousin. "Haven't you heard? She's taking some time off. Something about meeting the man of her dreams and wanting to spend some time with him. Probably before he comes to his senses," she added. Everyone at the hospital knew of Gloria's reputation.

"No, I hadn't heard." Alyx breathed a sigh of relief. "I hope for his sake, he's deaf. She's not the type to hold that sharp tongue of hers for long." Alyx turned toward Zane. "The offer to leave is still on the table," she told him.

He nodded, ready to take her up on it, then stopped. The orchestra was playing another slow song.

"Want the last dance?" he asked her.

She did, but she didn't want to take advantage of him. He'd been exceptionally kind tonight.

"That's okay. You've more than done your time," she told him.

Because there was no pressure, he laced his hand through hers and drew her back to the dance floor.

Out of the corner of his eye, as he placed his other hand to the small of her back, Zane saw Josef looking at them from across the room. The patriarch nodded his head in approval. Zane knew he should have resented it. Ordinarily, he would have. But this time around, he didn't.

He didn't bother exploring why.

Chapter 14

Standing at the foot of his bed, Alyx looked from her chart to the old man her hastily filled out paperwork was referring to.

Paramedics had brought him in less than an hour ago. They, like a good deal of the ER personnel, were on a first-name basis with the man.

Alvin Weinberg was not a new face at Patience Memorial.

Self-described as "eighty-four years young," the spry, amiable octogenarian had already turned up twice in the ER in the short period that she had been working at the hospital. She'd come to view him as the grandfather she'd never had.

Setting the chart down, Alyx appraised the man

in the hospital bed. He met her gaze head-on, the personification of innocence.

"What did we talk about the last time, Mr. Weinberg?" she asked him.

The old man's face contorted slightly as he pretended to think and come up empty. Alvin shook his head sadly. "I can't seem to remember." And then his expression turned wistful. "Your brain's so much younger than mine. I'm afraid that you can keep track of these things so much better than I can."

She knew he knew what she referred to, but because he was so likeable, she played the game. "We talked about making sure you took your blood-thinning medication." She nodded toward the chart she'd set down on the metal cabinet. "It says here that you told the nurse you ran out of medication."

"I did," he told her, shaking his head sadly, the picture of solemnity.

"The last time you were here," she reminded him, "I gave you a month's worth of free samples and wrote you a prescription for six months of refills." She didn't have to bother looking it up. Although she saw a lot of people during the course of her day, she distinctly remembered her interactions with Mr. Weinberg.

Alvin appeared properly contrite. "I know, and I'm sorry, but I don't remember where I put the prescription. The more I looked for it, the more nervous I got." As he spoke, he started making concentric circles on his chest, as if to illustrate his next point. "And then these funny little pains started in my chest…" He dropped his hand

and widened his eyes. "I called 911 right away because that's what you told me to do. So I did," he concluded with a flourish.

"I remember," she replied. She drew closer to him and took his hand, trying to connect with the elderly man and drive her point home. "This is serious, Mr. Weinberg. If you skip your medication, you could wind up getting a blood clot and die. You really need to remember to take your blood thinner," she said, emphasizing each word. "The medicine you take to keep your erratic heartbeat under control." She used the simple explanation rather than refer to the condition by its name, atrial fibrillation, because it might further confuse him. "It makes you more susceptible to blood clots, which is why you need to take the warfarin," Alyx concluded, using the medication's pharmaceutical name.

Alvin shook his head, a nineteenth-century man caught in a twenty-first-century world. "Why can't they make a medicine that doesn't have all those side effects?" he asked.

"Someday, they will," she promised, "but for now, you have to be careful not to skip your doses."

"I bet you could come up with medication without side effects if you put your mind to it," Alvin speculated with confidence as she made a few notations on the bottom of his chart. "You're a very bright girl. Like my granddaughter, Valerie. You remind me a lot of her, you know," he told her affectionately.

She knew. He'd told her that the last time he'd been here. She had a suspicion that Mr. Weinberg wasn't nearly as forgetful or absentminded as he pretended to be. Mr. Weinberg was lonely. His only son, Jason, had moved to Texas, taking his family with him. Alvin Weinberg, a lifelong New Yorker, had stubbornly remained behind. She was certain that he regretted it now, but, at eighty-four he probably felt he was too old to start over again somewhere new.

He was here just as much for the company as he was for the treatment. Maybe more.

She pocketed her pen and flipped the pages closed on the chart. "Well, it looks like we'll be keeping you overnight again for observation just to make sure that you're all right, Mr. Weinberg." She patted his hand to reassure the man that this was just a precaution.

Mr. Weinberg nodded, the few wisps of white hair he still had left moving in the slight breeze created by the air conditioning system.

"Will you be up to visit me?" he asked hopefully. "Like last time? Just to make sure I'm not in a coma or anything," he added for effect.

"Of course I'll be up to see you," she told him with a reassuring smile.

Alyx made it a point to look in on the patients she wound up admitting to the hospital. Medicine wasn't an anonymous discipline to her, but a hands-on career that required concern and total commitment. That meant treating the person, not the condition. Part of that entailed checking in on the patient to make sure that no new problems arose and that the existing ones were being handled and resolved.

Signaling Jaime, one of the orderlies working the floor on this shift, Alyx stepped back as he came into the small cubicle. "Time to whisk Mr. Weinberg upstairs to his room," she told Jaime. "Room 314."

Taking another step back, she bumped up against what felt like a rock-hard chest. That could only belong to one person.

Zane.

She turned around to face him, a grin instantly blooming on her lips. Always sunny, her countenance lit up even more. "What are you doing here?"

"I had some extra time," he told her. "So, because I was in the neighborhood, I thought I'd take you to lunch," he said, conveniently skipping the part where he'd bribed his partner to go eat somewhere else so he could use the squad car during lunch.

His ears perking up, Mr. Weinberg latched on to Zane's wrist as Jaime pushed the man and his bed into the main ER area. The journey came to a sudden halt. "Hey, you got a really good doctor there," the old man told him with enthusiasm. Unusually sharp blue-gray eyes gave him a very thorough once-over. "She your girl?" Alvin asked.

Alyx got between them and deftly disengaged the old man's hand from Zane's wrist. "I'll see you later, Mr. Weinberg," she said firmly.

"'Cause if she's not," Mr. Weinberg went on talking as if she hadn't said a word and the orderly wasn't pushing him toward the service elevator, "I'm staking my claim on her. Don't forget, Doc," the old man was almost shouting now as he twisted about to look at her. "You said you'd come by to see me later."

She laughed, shaking her head. "I won't forget," she called after him just before the service elevator doors shut, cutting off any further communication.

"Fan club?" Zane asked, raising an eyebrow in mild amusement.

"Mr. Weinberg? He's a sweet, lonely old man. His only son moved his family to Texas three years ago and now he has nobody. So he 'forgets' to take his medicine and gets brought in here every so often to socialize." She was very fond of the old man. "I'm sorry if he embarrassed you."

"Takes more than an old man daring me to stake a claim on the woman he adores to embarrass me," Zane told her, a very seductive smile slipped along his lips. She felt her heart do a little flip-flop. "So, are you free for lunch?"

She'd managed to clear her board this morning. This would be a perfect way to reward herself.

"Yes."

But even as she said the word, the two-way regulation issue radio clipped to Zane's belt emitted an unnerving, high-pitched sound. That was quickly followed by the voice of the dispatch desk asking if he heard her.

"But obviously you're not," Alyx concluded with a resigned laugh. She saw the reluctant look in his eyes. "Go." She waved him on.

Zane sighed and nodded as he removed the radio, pressed a button and listened to the instructions coming over the unit. The message was short, succinct. There was a three-car accident not many blocks away from the hospital.

"I've got a feeling you're going to be in on this, too," he remarked, breaking the connection.

There went lunch, Alyx thought. It wouldn't be the first time. And with the Dragon Lady still on her "love" vacation, they were short-handed. Happy, but short-handed.

"Are you coming by after five?"

The question had just popped out of her mouth on its accord.

Alyx knew she shouldn't ask, that asking made it sound as if she'd gotten used to his coming by the hospital to take her home. But the truth was, she *had* gotten used to his coming by. Not only that, but she looked forward to it even though she knew she shouldn't allow herself to take Zane's appearance in her life for granted.

With each passing day, there was less and less logical reason for Zane to continue to spend his off-duty hours "guarding" her from a man who, more than likely, had fled the country by now. Or at the very least, fled the state.

Zane nodded, hooking the unit back onto his belt. "I'll be by," he told her.

The next moment, he was gone. The effect he had on her lingered like a bright glow for the length of the afternoon. Even though she tried very hard not to get used to his presence, not to get used to seeing his face beside her every morning when she woke up, she knew damn well that she was sinking further and further into that tender trap. The one that held her heart captive.

She struggled against it, but there was nothing she could do. Certainly logic was no weapon. She was in love with Zane Calloway. In love with his strength, his dedication, his caring. She was even in love with the serious way he went about his responsibilities.

It wouldn't be easy, getting over this man when he finally slipped out of her life again.

Not easy? Alyx mocked herself. It would be damn near impossible. She wasn't the type to love easily—or to bounce back from that emotion easily either.

She couldn't recall *ever* feeling like this about anyone.

With a shake of her head, Alyx forced herself not to think about the future and the pain lurking in the shadows, waiting to consume her. There were a great many other things to occupy her mind than the aura of sadness that she knew would sink into her soul once Zane left her life.

She had seen a record number of patients today. All but Mr. Weinberg and a young mother of two who had an appendix on the verge of rupturing, had been sent home after treatment. She's certainly earned her meager paycheck today, she thought as she glanced at her watch. It was very close to the end of her shift. If no one came bursting through the ER doors in the next few minutes, she could start getting ready.

After she looked in on Mr. Weinberg the way she promised, she reminded herself.

No time like the present.

Rather than wait for the elevator, she hurried up the stairwell to the third floor.

"I was wondering when you'd get here," Mr. Weinberg said as she entered the room. His round face lit up like a Christmas tree.

"It's been a busy day," she told him.

He shook his head in sympathy. "They work you too hard," he told her. "How about that boyfriend of yours? He treat you well?"

"He's not my boyfriend, Mr. Weinberg," she told him patiently.

He chuckled. "Don't lie to an old man," he told her. "I see things. He has feelings for you. And you have feelings for him."

"Since when are you an old man?" she teased, changing the subject.

"Figure of speech," he corrected. Her pager went off. He frowned at it. "Don't they know you're going home?"

"No rest for the weary," she told him. With a sigh, she angled the pager at her waist to see who wanted her.

"Who is it?" Mr. Weinberg asked. He made no apology for his curiosity.

"It's from the hospital pharmacist. Something about the medication I requested being denied." She frowned. "I never requested any medication—other than the blood thinner for you," she said. And that had been sent up.

"Oh well, I'd better see what this is about. These things have a way of escalating and getting out of control unless they're nipped in the bud." She smiled affectionately at the old man and patted his deeply veined hand. "I'll see you first thing tomorrow—to discharge you."

"I'll be here," he promised her.

The pharmacist was probably going stir crazy, Alyx thought, this time taking the elevator. Cutbacks had forced the hospital to have only one pharmacist on duty at a time. Consequently, the man was alone for hours at a time in an eight-by-ten box of an office with no one to talk to. In his place, she'd be looking for reasons to get people to come in, too.

She hoped this wouldn't take long. She wanted to get to the lockers. That was their meeting place, hers and Zane's. Waiting for Zane to come was her favorite part of the day.

Well, *one* of her favorite parts of the day, she amended as she waited for several people to get off on the first floor. She loved waking up in the morning with him beside her, loved falling asleep at night with his arms around her. Loved every moment she spent with him. Even the silences were good.

She was the only one left on the elevator as the doors closed again. The elevator took her down to the basement.

Unlike the other floors, there was no one around when the doors opened. No one around in the immediate area either. One of the florescent lights was out, casting the hall more into darkness than light.

Alyx hurried down the corridor to the pharmacy, wanting to get this over with. Approaching the office, she glanced in through the glass enclosure.

The room was empty.

"Curiouser and curiouser," she murmured under her breath. Opening the door, Alyx walked in. "Hello? Drake?" She called the pharmacist's name. "It's Alyx Pulaski." There was no response. "You just paged me."

Maybe he'd changed his mind, she thought. Oh well, she'd tried. Time to go.

Turning toward the door, Alyx stopped dead. A pair of feet stuck out from behind a small, white table in the corner. She hurried over, not knowing what to expect, trying to be braced for anything.

The sight still startled her. The pharmacist was on the floor, unconscious and bleeding from what looked like a head wound. Had he fainted and hit his head? But the wound was in the front of his head and he was on his back. If he'd hit his forehead, wouldn't he have pitched forward?

Then why—

The next moment, a scream filled her lungs, but never had an opportunity to emerge. Instead, it throbbed in her throat like a stifled echo.

A hand tightly covered her mouth. So tightly she could hardly draw in a breath. Someone had come up behind her, clapped a hand over her mouth and roughly yanked her up to her feet.

The first disjointed thought that streaked across her

mind was that a junkie had broken in and she'd stumbled in on his attempt to rob the pharmacy.

She tried to peel his hand from her mouth. The arm around her waist tightened harder, feeling as if it were cutting her in two.

And then she heard his voice. Her blood froze in her veins the second she recognized it.

"Thought you'd get away with it, didn't you?" the deep voice taunted.

McBride.

How had he gotten in here? And what had he done to Drake? Was the man dead? She hadn't been able to check for a pulse before he grabbed her.

The next moment, his large hand still covering her mouth, McBride spun her around to face him. The look in his eyes was pure evil.

He seemed to relish the glimmer of fear she knew had to be evident in her eyes. She struggled to bank it down. "That's right. Me. I don't like leaving loose ends. And you, you bitch, you're a loose end." His smile was cold, threatening. "But not for long."

She jerked her head back. The sudden movement separated his hand from her mouth. "What do you want from me?"

"Same thing I wanted before. In the elevator that first morning. Remember? Your heart," he snapped when she made no answer. "Except this time, I want it on a platter. Literally," he emphasized. "Because you made me kill Abby before I was ready. Hell, I might not have even killed her. I really liked her. She did everything I told her to, was everything I needed her to be.

"But then you came along and ruined everything," he accused. "Talking to you made her mouthy. Abby told me you said she didn't have to put up with me. That she had the right to leave. To leave me," he yelled angrily, hitting his chest with his fist. "I showed her she didn't," he declared smugly. And then his eyes narrowed as he accused, "But that was your fault."

And he was here for revenge. She could see it in his face. He meant to kill her. She needed to stall. Someone *had* to come down here sooner or later. She had to keep him talking until then.

"Look, whatever you have planned, you're not going to get away with it—"

"Well, we won't know until I try, will we?" he laughed nastily.

The next moment, before she could say anything, McBride caught her completely off guard. Pulling back his arm, he punched her in the chin. He hit her so hard that he knocked her unconscious.

As she crumpled, McBride caught her. In one smooth motion, he slung her over his shoulder as if she weighed no more than a wet towel.

"Payback time," he announced, laughing.

Zane was early and he knew it. But he wanted to take her out to dinner to make up for the lunch he hadn't gotten a chance to share with her. Going out to dinner would surprise her, and he liked the way she looked when she was surprised. Pleasantly surprised, he amended.

He nodded at the receptionist at the ER admissions desk. The woman, Jillian, nodded back and automatically pressed the button to release the lock on the inner door that would allow him to come inside.

"She's not here," Jaime, the orderly who'd taken Mr. Weinberg up to his room earlier, told him as their paths crossed. "She was going to look in on Mr. Weinberg and then leave—unless she was waiting for you," the young man added with a grin.

Bad sign, Zane thought. They—he and Alyx—were looked upon as what his mother had once referred to as "an item." The people Alyx worked with were thinking of them as a couple. He was going to have to change that.

Soon.

But not yet.

"What room's the old man in?"

"I put him in 314," Jaime answered just before he rounded a corner to get a blanket from the supply closet for one of the patients.

Zane debated waiting by the lockers the way he usually did, but what if something came up in the interim? What if the old man—Weinberg, was it?—wouldn't stop talking? He decided his best bet was to go upstairs and let her know he was here.

"She's not here," Alvin Weinberg told him the moment Zane looked into the room.

He took a few steps in. "I can see that. Has she come to see you?"

"Sure she came," Weinberg said, rising to Alyx's defense. "The doc doesn't break promises the way my son does—"

The man gave every indication that he was about to launch into a long story. Zane cut him off before he could get started. "Do you know if she went to the lockers after she left you?"

Mr. Weinberg shook his head. "No. She got a page from the pharmacy. Something about a prescription not being filled. She said she had to go down to straighten it out. Cut our visit short," he complained.

"She'll make it up to you," Zane replied, hurrying out of the room.

He didn't bother with the elevator. Instead, Zane opened the door to the stairwell and quickly went down the four flights to the basement, his passage propelled by the uneasy feeling that had taken hold of his gut.

Something was off.

He couldn't put his finger on it, or even explain why, but he knew. And the feeling mushroomed, as did his sense of urgency, the closer he got to the basement.

Zane ran down the last flight of stairs.

Chapter 15

Was it just his imagination, or did it seem like every second light in the basement hallway was out or dimming?

It took Zane a moment to orient himself when he emerged out of the stairwell. He'd had no occasion to come down to the basement before. Scanning the walls and raising his eyes toward the ceiling, he searched for printed signs that would tell him which way to go to find the pharmacy.

The obvious one, the one for the cafeteria, was large enough for even people with severely impaired vision to be able to read. The way to the pharmacy was only indicated by a small sign composed of red letters across a white arrow. The arrow was pointing one hundred and eighty degrees away from the cafeteria. The hallway was empty in either direction. He seemed to have hit upon a lull.

Although it appeared that no one was around to hear him, instincts had Zane hurrying as quietly as possible. If she could see him now, Alyx would probably laugh at him—and he really hoped that she would because that would mean she was unharmed. That he was just being overly paranoid for no reason. He could live with that. Live with practically anything as long as Alyx was all right.

Why shouldn't she be? he silently demanded and then realized that some of her eternal optimism had obviously seeped into his brain. But after all, he reasoned, falling back on logic, there'd been no sightings of McBride since he'd suddenly disappeared. As apparently was his habit after "losing" a spouse or girlfriend.

Wiring Harry McBride's photograph—lifted from his last driver's license—to the various police departments that had been involved in the other abuse and assault cases he'd managed to dig up had gotten Zane the positive confirmation he'd been looking for. And it also established a pattern. McBride always took off after his dealings came to light. Whether it was abuse, or, in the Tennessee and Alabama cases, suspected murder, no one ever saw him again. And it was definitely McBride. Each department made a positive ID.

That information didn't exactly make Zane happy either, because although it established a pattern, it also meant that McBride was probably out there biding his time. Waiting to make the most of the element of surprise. And *that* meant that McBride could strike at any time, take his revenge against Alyx at any time.

The thought left him numb. Not to mention scared.

Zane wasn't accustomed to being scared. To his recollection, that was one of the emotions he'd successfully blocked out.

Until now.

Alyx had managed to upend a lot of things in his life.

Zane supposed that he would have to put in a little more time watching over Alyx, keeping her safe. As he rolled the thought over in his mind, he waited for the feeling of confinement to set in, which in turn would make him feel as if he was suffocating. Unable to breathe.

It amazed him that the feeling didn't materialize. Didn't even whisper across his mind.

But fear did.

He couldn't shake the feeling that she was in trouble. That she needed him.

Turning a corner, he thought he saw someone disappearing around the far end of the corridor. At the same time, he passed by the pharmacy. No one appeared to be inside the glass enclosure. Didn't that old man say she'd gone to talk to the pharmacist?

Then he saw the man lying on the floor behind the table.

Zane didn't stop, didn't go in to check on his condition. Instead, gut feelings told him to go after the guy he'd just seen disappear around the corner. Whoever it was hadn't been in hospital scrubs and he wasn't wearing a white lab coat. There was no reason for anyone who wasn't part of the staff to be down here in this part of the basement. There were nothing but a few supply closets on this end. No patients, no laboratories or rooms with radiology equipment. Just windowless rooms used for storage. Alyx had told him that the other day. He couldn't remember why the subject had come up.

A sense of urgency propelled him on.

Picking up speed, Zane started to run.

"Hey, you there," he called out. "Stop for a minute. I want to talk to you."

In response, he heard the sound of crepe soles squeaking against the vinyl flooring. Quickly.

Someone was running.

Running away from the sound of his voice.

Zane knew he had to catch the person before it was too late. If whoever he'd just glimpsed made it to the exit, all bets were off.

Pouring it on, Zane ran as if this was to be the race of his life. Because maybe it was.

Whoever he was chasing had Alyx, he could *feel* it in his bones.

"Stop, I'm a cop," Zane called out, his voice echoing down the winding corridor. Going around another corner, he saw his quarry.

McBride.

And the man had Alyx slung over his shoulder like dead weight.

Zane didn't even remember pulling out his weapon, but suddenly, there it was, in his hand. He took careful aim at McBride.

"Stop or I'll shoot," he warned.

McBride swung around. It was then that Zane saw he was brandishing a gun of his own.

"You do and her brains are going to be splattered all over this hall," McBride threatened. "My way, you put your gun up and she gets to live." The smile on his face turned malevolent. "At least for a little while. Now, drop the damn gun!" McBride barked.

Even at this distance, Zane could see that McBride's eyes made him look possessed. He wasn't in his right mind. There was no telling what the man would do, but he couldn't take a chance on provoking him.

"Don't hurt her, McBride," Zane called out to him. "Take me instead. Nobody's going to bother you if you have a cop as a hostage."

"Tempting," McBride said sarcastically, pretending to roll the idea over in his head, "but let's face it, you're not my type. Little doctor-do-gooder here," he hit her across the buttocks with the barrel of his gun for emphasis, "needs a lesson in humility, and I intend to give it to her, a number of times," he added, punctuating the promise with the kind of nasty laugh that made Zane's flesh crawl.

Zane's mind raced, searching for a viable way to save Alyx. If McBride managed to get out of the building with her, Alyx's chances of survival decreased a hundredfold.

The man undoubtedly had his car parked right outside the exit.

He couldn't be allowed to reach it.

Zane made up his mind. He was going to rush McBride even though he had no cover available to him, nothing to hide behind from here to there. No way to avoid being shot. But if he didn't try to rush McBride, the maniac would get away and there was no telling what he would do to Alyx before he killed her.

Bracing himself, Zane was about to charge into McBride, but before he could, McBride shrieked in surprised outrage. Piercing the air, the horrible sound ruptured the huge bubble of tension that throbbed about them.

Zane had no idea what was going on until he saw McBride drop Alyx. She sprang to her feet and hurled herself against her attacker, causing McBride to stagger backward and ram his back against the wall.

All Zane could think was that McBride was still holding his gun.

"Alyx, get away from him!" Zane shouted, sprinting the short distance that separated him from McBride.

But even as he yelled out the warning to her, McBride fired his weapon. The shot went wild. It completely missed Alyx who was angrily pounding on McBride with her fists. She landed several well-aimed blows across his chin and managed to knock McBride out.

All in all, she was one tough little cookie, Zane thought, steadying himself. A tough cookie who could have gotten herself killed.

"I'll take it from here, Alyx." Authority echoed in Zane's voice despite the fact that there was now a stinging pain running through him. But the pain was nothing in comparison to the way he'd felt just a few moments ago, when he thought McBride was going to pull off kidnapping Alyx.

Holding his gun trained on the crumpled figure on the floor, he gave Alyx a quick once-over. He didn't see any blood. "Are you okay?"

"I will be if you let me hit him a few more times," she told him, glaring at the unconscious man on the floor.

"You have to leave something for the judge to sentence," he told her with a relieved smile. "What the hell happened?" he asked. "How did he manage to get his hands on you and why did he just scream like that?"

"He had Drake—the pharmacist—page me. When I got there, Drake was on the floor, out cold. McBride got the jump on me and punched me in the face. I guess I passed out. I came to when he was yelling at you—and I bit his shoulder," she said matter-of-factly. "It was the only way I could think of to keep him from shooting you at point-blank range."

Relieved, amused, Zane started to laugh. But even as he did, the very act seemed to intensify the sharp darts of pain shooting through him. This wasn't a new pain. He'd felt this way before, he realized. Just recently when—

McBride suddenly scrambled to his feet as he uttered a guttural yell. At the same time, he lunged to grab Alyx again. What happened next was sheer reflex. Zane spun around and shot McBride in the chest. It was a single kill shot.

McBride was dead before he hit the floor.

The iron grip Alyx had managed to keep on her emotions cracked then. Although she tried hard not to, she could feel herself begin to shake. The horror of what could have happened echoed in her brain.

Relieved to be still standing, to have Zane still standing, she threw her arms around his neck.

"Oh God," she murmured into his shoulder, struggling to keep the sobs that were choking her from escaping. As she buried her face against his shoulder, she felt him wince.

Alyx instantly pulled back. "You're wounded," she cried, then raised her eyes to his face. "Again."

Zane glanced at his shoulder. There was a steady trickle of blood emerging now. That explained the stinging feeling. Initially he'd thought that it was just the wound he'd received last month acting up. Apparently not.

"Lucky for me you're so damn good at what you do." His shoulder was really beginning to ache now. Digging into his pants pocket with the wrong hand, he pulled out his cell phone and put in a call to the precinct for some backup.

The first to arrive on the scene, Detective Tony Santini, took one look at Zane's shoulder and told him to have it seen to.

"Like *now,* Calloway," he emphasized when Zane made no move to leave. "Sasha would have my head if I let you stand here, bleeding, while I asked you questions. Go. I'll take over here."

"Am I free to go with him?" Alyx wanted to know.

"I'm counting on it. You're the one who's got the needle with his name on it," Tony cracked. He made a point of waving both of them on. "I'll get your statements later," he promised, "when your body starts replacing all that blood you lost."

Zane didn't need any more than that. Taking Alyx's hand in his, he led the way to the elevator. He would have taken the stairs because it was only one flight, but he was beginning to feel just the slightest bit lightheaded.

The elevator arrived almost immediately. "That was pretty quick thinking on your part," Zane said as they got on the elevator. When she raised a quizzical eyebrow, he added, "Biting McBride like that."

She didn't even remember thinking about it. She just did it instinctively. "I was afraid McBride was going to shoot you. I had to do something."

He hit the button for the first floor. "He shot me anyway."

"But at least he didn't kill you," she pointed out as the doors closed. "I don't know what I would have done if he'd killed you."

The emotion he saw in her eyes stirred him, but he had no idea how to respond to what she'd just said.

Words had never come easily to him and he had no role models to emulate.

Zane shrugged his good shoulder. "You're resilient. You would have gone on."

Was he just dismissing her? Telling her there was nothing between them? She couldn't tell.

"If you say so," she replied flatly.

On the first floor now, they got off the elevator. Really struggling to keep the world in focus, Zane let Alyx take the lead.

Hurrying, worried about his arm, Alyx deliberately took the back way into the ER, avoiding the receptionist and whatever patients were out in the waiting room. She knew Zane would want his privacy more than ever now.

None of the rooms were empty, so she commandeered the first empty bed she came to. Telling Zane to sit down on the edge of the bed, she pulled shut the curtain that ran along the bed's perimeter. Getting the suturing kit ready took her all of a few moments.

"I'm beginning to know how to do this in my sleep," she commented as she went about the job of cleaning, sterilizing and then finally sewing up his wound. The bullet had mercifully gone clean through this time, doing away with the need to probe and hunt for it within his opened flesh.

As before, rather than turn his head away the way most people did, he watched her work. Fascinated. "I should keep you on retainer," Zane quipped. "Even with

McBride gone, there might be other times that I'll need you to be my angel of mercy."

She thought of a few of the women she'd graduated with. Most of them were still single. And Zane's looks were really hypnotic. He'd be snatched up within sixty seconds. "I'm sure that any number of doctors would fight for that right."

"I don't want any one of a number," he told her, twisting around so that he could look into her eyes. "I want you." When she stopped working and looked up at him, surprised by his blunt statement, he cleared his throat. "I mean, your work is good, you don't make these big, Frankenstein-type stitches—"

She laughed, shaking her head. "You can stop now. I get the picture."

For a moment, he watched her work in silence. "You know," he began without any preamble, "it's going to seem strange, not having to guard you anymore."

It was going to feel strange to her, too, not waking up to his face. Not looking forward to the end of the day because she would be ending it with him.

She did her best to sound cheerful as she worked. "Bet you're glad about that."

He raised his eyes to hers. They held for a moment. "You'd lose that bet," he told her quietly. Then before she could comment or ask any questions, he said, "Marry me, Alyx."

The needle she'd been using fell out of her hand, making a little tinny sound as it hit the tile and fell at her feet.

"Lucky for you I'm finished," she said, stooping down to retrieve the needle before someone wound up stepping on it and getting the needle embedded in the bottom of their shoe.

"'Lucky for you I'm finished' is not an answer," he finally said when she didn't say anything further.

She froze and looked at him. "I didn't think you expected one."

That didn't make any sense to him. "Don't people usually get answers to proposals?"

"Serious ones, yes."

He peered at her face as he asked, "What makes you think this isn't a serious proposal?"

"Because you're the one doing the asking." She couldn't see him asking any woman to marry him. He was too much of a free spirit. He'd told her so. And she'd believed him. "Just for future reference," she added as she began to clear away what was left of the suture kit, "boredom is a very poor reason to ask someone to marry you."

"I wasn't asking you to marry me because I was bored," he countered. "I was asking you to marry me because I love you."

For the second time in as many minutes, the needle, which she was just about to deposit into the hazardous waste container, slipped from her fingers and fell on the floor.

This time she didn't immediately bend down to pick it up. Instead, she stared at him, trying to understand. To focus. "Did you just say—?"

Suddenly feeling as eager as a teenager, he cut her off. "Yes, I did."

She frowned, looking at the empty syringe she'd just used before starting to stitch up his wound. "Funny, you didn't react like this to the local the last time I gave it to you."

"The injection has nothing to do with it," he told her flatly. "You, you have something to do with it. You have *everything* to do with it."

She deposited the syringe into the hazardous waste container, her eyes never leaving his face. She could always tell when someone was lying. "You're telling me you think you love me."

"No, I'm telling you I *know* I love you. I just had trouble admitting it to myself. Until I thought McBride was going to kidnap you right in front of me." Even saying it sent a cold shiver racing up and down his spine. "And then suddenly, I knew."

There had to be a punch line here somewhere, Alyx thought. She couldn't allow herself to be reeled in. "Knew what?"

He took her hand in his, stilling her movements. "That you were the only thing in my life that was keeping it from being empty. That I didn't want to go back to the way things were. That I wanted to spend the rest of my life guarding that body of yours—and selfishly saving it for me."

She was beginning to believe him.

Alyx took a deep breath, then let it out slowly. Her

eyes never left his face. "You're sure this isn't a reaction to the injection I just gave you?"

"This is a reaction to you," he corrected. "Now, if you need some time to process this, I understand." He did his best to sound patient, even though he was feeling anything *but* that right now. Rushing her could accomplish just the opposite of what he wanted. "You can have all the time you need to—"

"No."

The single, two-letter word was like a rapier pushed straight through his heart. He felt devastated—but still very unwilling to accept defeat so readily. "Maybe if you think about it, you won't turn me down."

She shook her head. He didn't understand, she thought. "I'm not turning you down, Zane," she told him. "I'm telling you that I don't need the extra time. I know what my answer is."

Suddenly there didn't seem to be enough air in the small cubicle. "And—?"

Her smile radiated from every part of her. "Do you have to ask?"

He needed to hear it, to hear her accept his proposal. To accept him. "I'm not nearly as confident as you think I am. Yes, I have to ask."

"Oh, for goodness' sakes, she's telling you yes. So kiss her and get it over with already!" a heavily accented, disembodied woman's voice on the other side of the curtain ordered impatiently. "What are you waiting for? Cue cards?"

Alyx grinned from ear to ear.

Leaning into him, she nodded toward the common side of the curtain and whispered, "The voice of wisdom has spoken."

"Certainly can't argue with that," Zane agreed.

Gathering her closer to him with his good arm, Zane brought his mouth down to hers and kissed her.

The curtain remained drawn and in place for a very long time.

* * * * *

COMING NEXT MONTH

Available February 22, 2011

#1647 OPERATION: FORBIDDEN
Black Jaguar Squadron
Lindsay McKenna

#1648 SPECIAL AGENT'S SURRENDER
Lawmen of Black Rock
Carla Cassidy

#1649 SOLDIER'S NIGHT MISSION
H.O.T. Watch
Cindy Dees

#1650 THE DOCTOR'S DEADLY AFFAIR
Stephanie Doyle

ROMANTIC SUSPENSE

REQUEST YOUR FREE BOOKS!

2 FREE NOVELS
PLUS
2 FREE GIFTS!

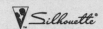

Sparked by Danger, Fueled by Passion.

YES! Please send me 2 FREE Silhouette® Romantic Suspense novels and my 2 FREE gifts (gifts are worth about $10). After receiving them, if I don't wish to receive any more books, I can return the shipping statement marked "cancel." If I don't cancel, I will receive 4 brand-new novels every month and be billed just $4.24 per book in the U.S. or $4.99 per book in Canada. That's a saving of at least 15% off the cover price! It's quite a bargain! Shipping and handling is just 50¢ per book in the U.S. and 75¢ per book in Canada.* I understand that accepting the 2 free books and gifts places me under no obligation to buy anything. I can always return a shipment and cancel at any time. Even if I never buy another book, the two free books and gifts are mine to keep forever.

240/340 SDN FC95

Name	(PLEASE PRINT)	
Address		Apt. #
City	State/Prov.	Zip/Postal Code

Signature (if under 18, a parent or guardian must sign)

Mail to the **Reader Service:**
IN U.S.A.: P.O. Box 1867, Buffalo, NY 14240-1867
IN CANADA: P.O. Box 609, Fort Erie, Ontario L2A 5X3

Not valid for current subscribers to Silhouette Romantic Suspense books.

Want to try two free books from another line?
Call 1-800-873-8635 or visit www.ReaderService.com.

* Terms and prices subject to change without notice. Prices do not include applicable taxes. Sales tax applicable in N.Y. Canadian residents will be charged applicable taxes. Offer not valid in Quebec. This offer is limited to one order per household. All orders subject to credit approval. Credit or debit balances in a customer's account(s) may be offset by any other outstanding balance owed by or to the customer. Please allow 4 to 6 weeks for delivery. Offer available while quantities last.

Your Privacy—The Reader Service is committed to protecting your privacy. Our Privacy Policy is available online at www.ReaderService.com or upon request from the Reader Service.

We make a portion of our mailing list available to reputable third parties that offer products we believe may interest you. If you prefer that we not exchange your name with third parties, or if you wish to clarify or modify your communication preferences, please visit us at www.ReaderService.com/consumerschoice or write to us at Reader Service Preference Service, P.O. Box 9062, Buffalo, NY 14269. Include your complete name and address.

SRS11

USA TODAY *bestselling author Lynne Graham*
is back with a thrilling new trilogy
SECRETLY PREGNANT, CONVENIENTLY WED

Three heroines must marry alpha males to keep
their dreams…but Alejandro, Angelo and Cesario
are not about to be tamed!

Book 1—JEMIMA'S SECRET
Available March 2011 from Harlequin Presents®.

JEMIMA yanked open a drawer in the sideboard to find Alfie's birth certificate. Her son was her husband's child. It was a question of telling the truth whether she liked it or not. She extended the certificate to Alejandro.

"This has to be nonsense," Alejandro asserted.

"Well, if you can find some other way of explaining how I managed to give birth by that date and Alfie not be yours, I'd like to hear it," Jemima challenged.

Alejandro glanced up, golden eyes bright as blades and as dangerous. "All this proves is that you must still have been pregnant when you walked out on our marriage. It does not automatically follow that the child is mine."

"'I know it doesn't suit you to hear this news now and I really didn't want to tell you. But I can't lie to you about it. Someday Alfie may want to look you up and get acquainted."

"If what you have just told me is the truth, if that little boy does prove to be mine, it was vindictive and extremely selfish of you to leave me in ignorance!"

Jemima paled. "When I left you, I had no idea that I was still pregnant."

"Two years is a long period of time, yet you made no attempt to inform me that I might be a father. I will want DNA tests to confirm your claim before I make any decision about what I want to do."

"Do as you like," she told him curtly. "*I* know who Alfie's father is and there has never been any doubt of his identity."

"I will make arrangements for the tests to be carried out and I will see you again when the result is available," Alejandro drawled with lashings of dark Spanish masculine reserve.

"I'll contact a solicitor and start the divorce," Jemima proffered in turn.

Alejandro's eyes narrowed in a piercing scrutiny that made her uncomfortable. "It would be foolish to do anything before we have that DNA result."

"I disagree," Jemima flashed back. "I should have applied for a divorce the minute I left you!"

Alejandro quirked an ebony brow. "And why didn't you?"

Jemima dealt him a fulminating glance but said nothing, merely moving past him to open her front door in a blunt invitation for him to leave.

"I'll be in touch," he delivered on the doorstep.

What is Alejandro's next move? Perhaps rekindling their marriage is the only solution! But will Jemima agree?

*Find out in Lynne Graham's
exciting new romance
JEMIMA'S SECRET*

*Available March 2011
from Harlequin Presents®.*

Start your Best Body today
with these top 3 nutrition tips!

1. **SHOP THE PERIMETER OF THE GROCERY STORE:** The good stuff—fruits, veggies, lean proteins and dairy—always line the outer edges of the store. When you veer into the center aisles, you enter the temptation zone, where the unhealthy foods live.

2. **WATCH PORTION SIZES:** Most portion sizes in restaurants are nearly twice the size of a true serving and at home, it's easy to "clean your plate." Use these easy serving guidelines:
   - Protein: the palm of your hand
   - Grains or Fruit: a cup of your hand
   - Veggies: the palm of two open hands

3. **USE THE RAINBOW RULE FOR PRODUCE:** Your produce drawers should be filled with every color of fruits and vegetables. The greater the variety, the more vitamins and other nutrients you add to your diet.

Find these and many more helpful tips in

YOUR BEST BODY NOW
by
TOSCA RENO
WITH STACY BAKER

Bestselling Author of
THE EAT-CLEAN DIET®

Available wherever books are sold!

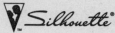

Silhouette®

ROMANTIC
SUSPENSE

Sparked by Danger, Fueled by Passion.

CARLA CASSIDY
Special Agent's Surrender

There's a killer on the loose in Black Rock,
and former FBI agent Jacob Grayson isn't about
to let Layla West become the next victim.

While she's hiding at the family ranch under Jacob's
protection, the desire between them burns hot.
But when the investigation turns personal,
their love and Layla's life are put on the line,
and the stakes have never been higher.

A brand-new tale of the

LAWMEN
of BLACK ROCK

Available in March wherever books are sold!

Visit Silhouette Books at www.eHarlequin.com

SRS27718